★ ★

SATURDAYS
WITH
HITCHCOCK

★ ★

★ ★

SATURDAYS WITH HITCHCOCK

★ ★

ELLEN WITTLINGER

Charlesbridge

For Morgan, beloved uncle to Rose and Jane,
and in memory of my own Uncle Walt,
never forgotten

Published by Charlesbridge
85 Main Street • Watertown, MA 02472 • (617) 926-0329
www.charlesbridge.com

Library of Congress Cataloging-in-Publication Data
Names: Wittlinger, Ellen, author.
Title: Saturdays with Hitchcock/Ellen Wittlinger.
Description: Watertown, MA: Charlesbridge, [2017] |
Summary: Twelve-year-old Maisie feels that she has enough
complications in her life: her actor uncle has moved in with her family
while he recovers from an accident and her father is not pleased, her
grandmother is slipping into dementia but wants to remarry, her mom
has been laid off, and her best friend, Cyrus, with whom she spends
Saturdays watching classic movies, has revealed that he is gay—but
Gary, the boy he has a crush on, seems more attracted to Maisie herself.
Identifiers: LCCN 2016043039 (print) | LCCN 2016048733 (ebook) |
ISBN 9781580897754 (reinforced for library use) | ISBN 9781607349976 (ebook)
Subjects: LCSH: Motion pictures—Juvenile fiction. | Actors—Juvenile fiction. |
Best friends—Juvenile fiction. | Friendship—Juvenile fiction. | Gays—Juvenile
fiction. | Families—Juvenile fiction. | Grandmothers—Juvenile fiction. |
Dementia—Juvenile fiction. | CYAC: Motion pictures—Fiction. | Actors and
actresses—Fiction. | Best friends—Fiction. | Friendship—Fiction. | Gays—
Fiction. | Family life—Fiction. | Grandmothers—Fiction. | Dementia—Fiction.
Classification: LCC PZ7.W7817 Sat 2017 (print) | LCC PZ7.W7817 (ebook) |
DDC 813.54 [Fic]—dc23
LC record available at https://lccn.loc.gov/2016043039

Printed in the United States of America
(hc) 10 9 8 7 6 5 4 3 2 1

Display type set in Canvas Inline and Canvas Icons
Text type set in New Century Schoolbook
Color separations by Coral Graphic Services, Inc., in Hicksville, New York, USA
Printed by Berryville Graphics in Berryville, Virginia, USA
Production supervision by Brian G. Walker
Designed by Susan Mallory Sherman and Sarah Richards Taylor

"Everything I learned, I learned
from the movies."
—Audrey Hepburn

"Hey, you kids!" Mr. Schmitz yells up at us. "Yeah, I'm lookin' at you. The movie's over. Go home!"

I lean over the balcony. "We're just talking."

"Well, talk outside. I wanna close up."

I shut my notebook, and Cyrus and I shuffle downstairs to the lobby. Mr. Schmitz is standing by the big double doors, a broom in his hand.

"How come you're only open afternoons?" Cyrus asks him.

"'Cause nobody comes downtown at night anymore. At night they wanna go to the multiplex at the mall." The way he says "multiplex" sounds like he means "hellmouth."

Not that many people go to the Lincoln Theater in the daytime either. There's only one screen, and Mr. Schmitz likes to show mostly old movies.

Which is fine with me. Sometimes, on Saturdays, Cyrus and I are the only people in the whole place.

We do go to the mall once in a while. We saw *The Martian* there, and *Inside Out*, which we both loved, but the mall is too much about buying stuff. Cyrus and I never have money for much more than the film anyway, so we like a place where going to the movies is pretty much all you *can* do. Besides, we can't even see PG-13 movies, a classification we're about six months away from. Old movies aren't like that—they were made for everybody.

We're probably Mr. Schmitz's best customers, but he's not particularly nice to us. He always acts like he's annoyed he has to rip our tickets in half, like why are we making him go to all that trouble? And if we want popcorn, his eyes roll back in his head before he shovels some into a box.

We don't mind too much, though. I figure he knows more about movies than anybody else in New Aztec, Illinois, because he always shows the best ones. I'm probably second smartest about movies. Cyrus comes in third because he just doesn't put enough time into it. Of course, my uncle Walt would beat us all if he still lived here, but he's out in Los Angeles, because that's where you have to live if you're a screen actor.

We wave to Mr. Schmitz as we push through the glass doors, and he grunts at us.

"We got a good crowd today, huh, Maisie?" Cyrus says, as if the Lincoln Theater belongs to us.

"*Casablanca* always gets a crowd," I say. "All the old people come."

"Yeah, old people and us. What's the matter with everybody else in this town?"

I shrug. "For some reason they think their actual lives are more interesting than movies. Which might be true if they lived someplace else."

"Like Morocco," Cyrus says. "I love that speech where Bogart says the problems of three people don't amount to anything compared to the problems of the world."

"Three *little* people," I correct him.

"Right."

"Of course the writing is good," I say, "but what I love about *Casablanca* is the lighting."

Cyrus snorts. "That's all you ever care about. The *lighting*."

"That's not true. And anyway, lighting is one of the most important elements of film."

Cyrus wrinkles up his nose. "I don't want to do lighting, Maze. I want to be a director. I want to be the *boss*."

"If you're going to be a director, you have to know this stuff, Cy. Remember how the vines and plants throw deep shadows up on the walls in *Casablanca*?"

"So?"

"That's Rembrandt lighting. The dark, twisted shadows echo how the characters' situations are tangled together and complicated."

"You just read that somewhere."

"Of course I read it somewhere! And we've talked about it too, how bright lights and heavy shadows are exaggerated for emotional effect."

"Okay, okay. Just because I don't remember every little thing about lighting . . ." He socks me lightly on the arm and I return his punch, but we're smiling. Cyrus and I never really argue.

We unlock our bikes from the parking meter out front and start pedaling home. There's not much traffic in downtown New Aztec on a Saturday. Everybody is either at the mall or locked in their air-conditioned houses. It's only the middle of May, but here in the Mississippi River valley it gets hot and steamy early.

In five minutes my bangs are sticking to my sweaty forehead, but at least my hair is short, so I can feel a little breeze on my neck. I'm practically the only girl in the sixth grade who doesn't have long hair, but those massive hair blankets are hot and heavy, and I don't see the point. I guess boys like girls to have long locks to swing around, but I don't care what boys think. Except for Cyrus, of course, and he doesn't care what I look like. We've been friends for so long that Cy probably doesn't even *notice* what I look like anymore.

"Let's go to my house," I say. "Mom has Dr Pepper."

Cyrus doesn't argue. His mother has banned all sugary beverages from the premises at their place, diet or otherwise, so he has to get his fix at my house. Which is easy enough, since I've lived across the street from him my whole life.

We let our bikes fall on the backyard lawn, which I'll get yelled at for later, but it's so hot and we're thirsty. The minute I open the kitchen door, though, I can hear my parents arguing in the living room, and I shush Cyrus. The only way a person gets any information about what's going on around here is by eavesdropping.

Dad sounds aggravated. "I thought he had a girlfriend out there in Hollyweird. Can't she take care of him?"

"They broke up months ago," Mom says.

"Can't he stay with your mother?"

"On that old foldout couch in her back room? That would be torture," Mom says. I'm daring to hope I know who they're talking about.

"Well, he can't expect you to be his nursemaid! You've got a job!"

"I know that, Dennis. Don't get mad at *me*. I didn't invite him!"

I hear the springs squeak as Mom flops into a chair. "Don't you have somewhere to be? Isn't your bowling team practicing today?"

"We've got a game tonight," Dad says. I can hear him pacing. "Look, it's not that I don't like the guy," Dad says. "It's just that every time he comes back here, you get all upset, and you end up taking it out on the rest of us."

"I do not. I get upset with my *mother*, is all. The way she flutters around him like he's the famous movie star he thinks he is—'Wade Wolf'—and not just her useless son, Walter Hoffmeister."

I turn to Cyrus and clap my hands silently. "My uncle Walt's coming!" I whisper.

He gives me a thumbs-up. I'm excited about Uncle Walt visiting, of course, but not so thrilled about my parents arguing over it. Mom has been known to snarl when she's angry, and while Dad usually stays calm and talks her down, that's not happening today.

"How on earth did he manage to break his collarbone, anyway?" Dad asks Mom. *What?*

"Doing a stunt in some movie. Collarbone and two ribs."

I pop around the corner in spite of myself. "Uncle Walt's hurt? What happened?"

Behind me Cyrus salutes my parents. He always does that, for a joke, when they're in their uniforms. My dad's a mail carrier, and my mom is a parking enforcement officer. They don't have any badges or medals or guns or anything.

"Oh, Maisie, I didn't hear you come in," Mom says. "He'll be okay. He just needs someplace to rest up while he heals."

"And somebody to wait on him hand and foot," Dad mutters to his shirtsleeve.

"How'd he get hurt?" I ask.

Mom sighs. "He jumped off a high diving board in some silly movie—"

"Probably *Girls Gone Haywire* or some great work of art like that," Dad grumbles.

"—and apparently he hit the low board beneath him," Mom continues. "I don't even see how that's possible, but—"

"Does that mean he can't finish the rest of the movie?" I ask.

"I'm sure it does," Dad says. "They're not going to hold up filming for six weeks just because some second-string actor got banged up."

"He's not a second-string actor," I say. "He was Eddie in *Sometime Tomorrow*."

"One decent role in ten years doesn't make him a movie star. Besides, eleven people saw that movie." Dad heads for the kitchen to get himself his work-is-over beer.

Cyrus laughs, and I elbow him in the side. He

thinks my dad's funny because his own father is so boring, but nobody laughs at my uncle Walt.

"*Sometime Tomorrow* got a rave review in the *Hollywood Reporter*," I call after Dad, "and *Entertainment Weekly* said Uncle Walt was an exciting new talent."

Dad calls back. "That was five years ago. He's older now and a lot less exciting."

"He actually had a pretty good part in this movie," Mom says. "He was a swimming instructor who falls in love with Kristen Bell."

Wow. "Kristen Bell from *Veronica Mars*? That's huge!"

Cyrus has been eating peanuts from the can Dad left open on the coffee table, but this gets his attention. "Cool! I love Kristen Bell. She was the voice of Anna in *Frozen* too."

"Never heard of her," Dad says as he walks back in. Which doesn't surprise me. Dad's not a movie person, and most of the TV he watches involves men trying to keep some kind of a ball away from each other.

"Anyway," Mom says, "I'm picking him up at the airport tomorrow at noon. And I don't think we can make him sleep on that awful couch in the den with all his broken bones."

"He can have my room!" I yell. "I'll sleep in the den!"

Dad laughs. "You've got the only air-conditioned room in the house, and you're giving it up? You'd do just about anything for that guy, wouldn't you?"

"Of course I would!"

Mom shakes her head. "Just like your grandmother."

Mom lets me ride along to the St. Louis airport to pick up Uncle Walt. We park the car and go inside to wait for him because he can't carry anything with his busted collarbone. I'm almost afraid to see what he looks like, all broken. Normally he's tall and strong and walks so fast I can't keep up.

I shriek a little the minute I see him heading toward us.

"Don't jump on him or hug him!" Mom warns.

"I *know*." Sometimes she treats me like an idiot.

He doesn't look as bad as I thought he might, but he's walking very slowly and carefully, and his face looks pale. He holds his upper body stiff, not moving his right arm, and I can see a bandage peeking out from below his shirt collar. He's got on this slouchy felt hat, and he reminds me of Indiana Jones in *Raiders of the Lost Ark*—after he's just gotten out of the snake pit.

As soon as he sees us, Uncle Walt starts smiling his usual enormous smile. It's not like anybody else's smile—it takes over his whole face and makes you feel like he's thrilled to see you. He's really good-looking too, with dark wavy hair that flops down onto his forehead. I don't know why he isn't a huge star—his smile alone should have made it happen. If he was older, he could have played Butch Cassidy or the Sundance Kid. He's that cool.

I get to him first, but I'm not sure what to do. Normally I'd leap on him, and he'd catch me and twirl me around. Instead he just ruffles my hair with his left hand.

"Are you okay?" I ask him.

"Don't worry, my dear. It's just a flesh wound," he says in a silly British accent. This is a reference to *Monty Python and the Holy Grail*, which we watched together the last time he was here. At least he hasn't lost his sense of humor.

He bends down a little, as if he wants to hug me, but I can tell it hurts him to do that, so I just put my arm around his waist and lean my head gently against his side. Mom gives him an air-hug, which is about all he'd get from her even if he wasn't hurt.

"Thanks for coming to get me, Cindy." He puts his arm around her waist for a minute, but she pulls away.

"Glad you made it." She doesn't sound all that glad.

"Wasn't the best flight I've ever had. Those seats are uncomfortable enough when you *don't* have broken bones."

"Can you explain to me, Walter, how somebody can jump off a high dive and hit the board below him with his shoulder?" Right away she acts like she's mad at him.

He winks at her, and his great grin sneaks out around the pain. "I guess I'm flexible." But Mom keeps her mouth in a flat line as we head for the luggage carousel.

"What's the name of the movie?" I ask. "Mom said Kristen Bell is in it. Is she as nice as she seems?"

"Nicer. And very funny. Didn't I email you? I meant to. The movie's called *Runaway*."

Uncle Walt always thinks he's told me things that he hasn't. He gets busy and forgets. "Who do you play?" I ask.

"I'm a swimming instructor who falls in love with Kristen's character when I'm giving lessons to her little boy. Well, I *was* the swimming instructor. I heard they got Milo Ventimiglia to do it now."

"I love him! He was in *Heroes*! And *Gilmore Girls*!" I say.

"You watch too much television, Maisie," Mom says. This is about the two-hundred-and-eleventh time she's said this to me, so I put her on mute. It's not even true. I watch a lot more movies than TV shows. Not that I don't like TV; I do. Uncle Walt got me a Netflix subscription so I could watch older stuff like *Freaks and Geeks* and *The X-Files*. But you can't watch TV on an enormous screen from the balcony of a huge room with your feet up on the seat in front.

"It must have been a pretty big part if they're giving it to Milo," I say.

"Medium big," Uncle Walt says. "It could have been my breakout role."

"You broke out, all right." Mom smirks at her own joke.

"At least now you get to visit us for a while," I say. "You didn't come for Christmas this year. We haven't seen you in ages."

"I know, but, hey, you liked my present, right?"

Uncle Walt sent me a small handheld video camera, just about the best present I could ever imagine.

"Oh my God! I love it so much!" I say. "Cyrus and I have already made a bunch of short videos, and we're planning to write a screenplay for a longer movie."

"It was too extravagant a gift for a child," Mom

says. I don't know why she always has to ruin things with her crabbiness.

"It wasn't that expensive," Uncle Walt says. "Besides, who else do I have to buy stuff for? At least Maisie appreciates the things I give her. I bought Courtney a bracelet she wanted, and she broke up with me anyway. If I'd known she was gonna dump me on New Year's Eve, I wouldn't have stayed in LA for the holidays."

"Why would anybody dump *you*?" I ask.

"Yeah, why would they?" Mom says. "An unemployed actor who waits tables for a living. Every girl's dream."

I can't believe it. Uncle Walt is barely off the plane, he's injured and in pain, and Mom *still* can't stop running him down. "He's not unemployed! He's an actor between jobs," I say.

Uncle Walt laughs good-naturedly. "Well, your mom's right that it's more or less the same thing. Until you get your big break."

"But you're in a movie with Kristen Bell. That's big!"

"*Was* in a movie," he says. "Past tense. I really blew it this time." He winces and moves his neck in a circle, as if it hurts.

The carousel whooshes to life, and bags start tumbling out.

"Here it comes. That blue duffel," Uncle Walt

says. "I'm afraid I'll have to ask you to carry it, Cindy."

"I know." Mom grabs the bag when it comes close, and heaves it up over the side of the conveyer belt. "Jeez, what's in here? Rocks?"

"Gold doubloons," Uncle Walt says, winking at me. "That's how they paid us on the last *Pirates of the Caribbean* movie." He didn't have any lines, but he was the pirate who accidentally knocked Jack Sparrow overboard. Cyrus and I saw it three times.

Mom hoists the bag onto her shoulder and starts walking all bent over. "Why can't you get a wheeled suitcase like a normal person?"

"Because he doesn't want to be a normal person," I say. "Right, Uncle Walt?"

"Right, Hitchcock." He always calls me that, ever since I told him two years ago that Alfred Hitchcock was my favorite director. Actually these days I'm more into Howard Hawks and Wes Anderson, but I still like Hitchcock and I love the nickname. I'd probably like any name Uncle Walt gave me.

He rests his left hand on top of my head as we slowly follow Mom out to the parking garage. I'm sorry he's hurt and everything, but I'm so glad he's here. His hand on my head feels like it's steering me. As always, Uncle Walt points me in the right direction.

Grandma is waiting at our house. The minute the car pulls into the driveway, she throws open the front door and comes running out.

"Walter!" she screams as we open the car doors. It takes Uncle Walt a minute or so to figure out how to hoist himself out of the front seat with the least amount of pain, but Grandma can't wait. He's barely upright before she's trying to hug him.

"Ma!" Mom yells. "Don't squeeze him, for God's sake. He's got broken ribs!"

"Hey, Ma," Uncle Walt says, grimacing. "Careful there."

"Oh, sweetheart, you're home!" Grandma says, tears running down her cheeks. "Please tell me you're back for good. Those movies are no good for you! They're killing you!"

"Ma, calm down. I just broke a few things."

"It's a sign you should stay here now. With us. If Cindy hadn't moved me into that little condo-minium place, you could stay with me."

Mom sighs as she holds open the front door, but she doesn't say anything.

"I thought you *wanted* to sell your big old house, Ma," Uncle Walt says gently. Even I re-member when that happened. She couldn't wait to get into a condo where somebody else was in charge of fixing the plumbing and mowing the grass.

"Well," Grandma continues, pushing Uncle Walt into the house, "at least Cindy and Dennis have room for you here."

"Not *forever*, we don't," Mom says. "Maisie has to sleep in the den."

"Hitch," Uncle Walt says, "you're my hero."

"I don't mind," I assure him. I would sleep in the garage if it meant Uncle Walt could stay longer. In the garage underneath the car, even. Of course, I don't want him to stay here forever like Grandma does. I want him to go back to Holly-wood and get his breakout role and be famous. I want his dreams to come true.

"Oh, who needs a *den*?" Grandma says. "What do you do in a den, anyway?"

"My piano is in the den," Mom says. "There's no other place—"

★17★

But Grandma isn't listening. Whenever Uncle Walt is around, he's the only one Grandma seems to be able to hear.

"Sit down!" she orders him. "Cindy, go get him a beer or something. You want a beer, honey?"

Uncle Walt sits carefully in a big chair and looks up at Mom. "Sure. That would be great if you've got one, Cin."

"It's barely two o'clock in the afternoon," Mom says.

"He's *hurt!*" Grandma yells. "Get him what he wants!"

Mom throws up her hands and stalks out of the room. "Sorry. I forgot for a minute that His Majesty, Prince Walter the Great, had returned. His wish is my command." Even though Mom acts like it's Uncle Walt she's mad at, it's really Grandma, I think. Nobody gets on Mom's last nerve faster than Grandma does.

I perch on the arm of his chair, and Uncle Walt winks at me. "Hey, Cindy," he calls to Mom, "it doesn't have to be a beer. Iced tea is fine too. Just something to wet my whistle."

There's a knock on the front door, and I know who it is. Cyrus was probably watching for our car to pull into the driveway.

"Come in!" I holler.

"Maisie, get up and answer the door," Mom says.

She hands Uncle Walt his beer without really looking at him.

But by the time I get to my feet, Cyrus has already opened the door and walked in. And then I see who's with him. Ugh. It's Gary Hackett. Wouldn't you know? It's like he's Cy's stalker these days.

"Um, Gary was at my house," Cyrus says. "He wanted to know if he could come over too."

"Hi, Maisie," Hackett says.

I glare at Hackett, but I speak to Cy. "Why'd he ask you if he could come to my house?"

"Maisie! You're being very rude," Mom says. "Come on in, Gary. Hi, Cyrus. Would you boys like something to drink?"

"Dr Pepper?" Cyrus looks hopeful. Hackett just nods like a bobblehead doll.

"I think I've still got some." Mom turns around and goes back to the kitchen.

"Can I have some too?" I call after her.

"You can get your own."

I follow Mom into the kitchen, though I hate to leave Cyrus and Hackett in there with Uncle Walt for long. The only thing Hackett wants to talk about lately is the movie *Blade Runner*, and I don't want him to get Uncle Walt all tired out talking about science fiction movies, which he and I don't even like that much. There's not enough Dr

Pepper left, so I just get myself a glass of water and race back into the living room.

Too late.

"You're lucky you live in Los Angeles," Hackett says. "I love how LA looks in *Blade Runner*. All rainy and gloomy and weird." He's sitting on the edge of the couch, leaning way over into Uncle Walt's airspace.

"It doesn't really look like that," I say. "It's hot and sunny most of the time."

"I know."

"Why do you always want to talk about that one movie?"

"I can talk about other stuff," he says. "I just like talking about *Blade Runner*."

"Well, maybe my uncle doesn't," I say.

Uncle Walt winks at me. "Ease up, Hitch. It's fine."

I'm not sure why Hackett bothers me so much these days. He's been in school with Cy and me for years. We played together sometimes when we were little kids, but the past few weeks he's been hanging around Cy all the time, and it's really annoying. Cyrus is too nice a person to ignore him, so I have to put up with him too. Also, Hackett's gotten really tall all of a sudden, which is weird because now I have to look up to him, which I don't like. He doesn't seem like the same kid he used to be. These days he reminds me of Logan Lerman in *The Perks of Being a Wallflower*, a movie I didn't think I'd like, but then I did.

I'm kind of on the short side, and I look like—well, imagine Alyson Hannigan in her *Buffy the Vampire Slayer* days, only with short brown hair. Anyway, I'm used to Cyrus, who's about the same height as me and looks kind of like Noah Hathaway, who played Atreyu in *The NeverEnding Story*, which has been one of our favorite movies since forever. I always feel *right* with Cyrus, but when Hackett's around, everything feels different. Off balance.

Uncle Walt's good arm is trapped in both of Grandma's hands. She's pulled her chair so close to his that she's practically tipping over into his lap.

"You've seen *Blade Runner*, haven't you?" Hackett asks Uncle Walt.

"Oh, sure," he says. "I liked it." I'm sure he didn't. He's just being nice.

And then Cyrus jumps in. "Do you think Deckard was really a replicant too? I don't think he—"

"Yes, he was!" Hackett yells. "There are clues all through the movie!" This is their favorite argument and one of the reasons I don't like to hang around with Hackett. He gets Cyrus talking about stuff I'm not even interested in.

"Who cares?" I say. "It's a dumb movie! I mean, what's that stupid unicorn doing in the middle of it, anyway?"

Hackett starts to open his mouth to answer me, and I realize I've made a serious mistake by asking a question. Fortunately Mom interrupts him.

"Since you've got an audience already," she says to Uncle Walt, "I'm going into my useless den to play the piano."

"Okay. Thanks again, Cin."

Mom grunts and disappears. I can see Hackett is dreaming up another idiotic question for Uncle Walt, but this time Grandma derails him.

"Walter, you should go lie down and rest," she says, petting Uncle Walt's arm like it's a small animal. "This has been a tiring day for you. I'll tuck you in and then go on home and see what Art's up to. I don't know why he didn't come with me this afternoon."

The room goes quiet and nobody moves. Uncle Walt looks up at me, and his eyes ask a question I can't answer. Art was my grandpa, and he's been dead for three years.

Grandma shakes her head as if she's trying to get everything to fall back into the right place. "Oh, my goodness, what am I talking about? Art's gone, isn't he?" She looks embarrassed and sad at the same time. "I forgot. Just for a minute. Isn't that silly?"

Uncle Walt takes her hand in his. "Happens to the best of us," he says, smiling. But it's not his easy smile, his gorgeous one. It's a tight, scared smile, like the one I'm forcing onto my face too.

Just then Mom starts banging away on the piano in the next room, playing "Tomorrow" from the musical *Annie*. She's an excellent piano player and sometimes plays for weddings, but today she's pounding those keys as if she's hammering them into place. The sound bounces off the walls of the quiet living room.

I'm trying to think of a way to turn the conversation away from my grandma's weird forgetful moment (without getting it back onto *Blade Runner* either) when Grandma starts crying. Which is also weird because Grandma never cries, and now she's done it twice in the last hour.

"I miss your daddy, Walter. I get so lonely sometimes." She grabs Uncle Walt around the neck in a crooked hug, and he lets out a surprised yelp.

Cyrus stands up and pulls Hackett by the back of his shirt collar. He wants to get them both out of here fast, and I don't blame him. If I didn't live here, I'd run for it too. But Hackett's not quite on his feet when Cy gives him a jerk toward the door, and he trips on the chair leg and knocks over the coffee table, sending a glass of beer and two Dr Peppers flying through space.

Which is when Dad walks through the front door. The coffee table's lying on its side; Hackett's hopping around on one foot, groaning; Grandma's crying onto Uncle Walt's sore shoulder; Uncle Walt's eyes are popping out of his head from pain; and Mom is musically looking forward to tomorrow as if she can't *wait* for this day to be over.

Dad shakes his head. "I knew I should have stayed at the bowling alley."

At least the spilled-drinks mess gives us kids something to do besides stare at Grandma. I run to get some rags from the utility room while Cy and Hackett pick up the coffee table and the empty glasses.

Mom stops playing for a minute and calls out, "Is anybody bleeding out there or going to the hospital?"

"No," I yell back.

She stays in the den and launches into "It's a Fine Life," the song the ragamuffin pickpockets sing in *Oliver!* I guess she's into orphans today.

Uncle Walt fills Dad in, sort of, on why Grandma's crying. "She got a little confused about Pop. I guess all the commotion about my accident tired her out."

"Yeah, that's tired us *all* out," Dad says, then turns to Grandma. "Evelyn, let me drive you home, okay? You can lie down a little while."

She finally lets go of her choke hold on Walt's neck, and the crying tapers off. "He was a good man, Art was," she says. "Picky about his mealtimes, though. Five o'clock, he wanted to eat supper."

"I remember," Dad says as he gets her to her feet and puts an arm around her waist.

"I don't miss that part," Grandma says. She rallies and shakes Dad off. "I'm not an invalid, Dennis. I can walk to the car by myself." Dad gives a quiet laugh. He always says Mom gets her feistiness from Grandma.

"Walter," Grandma continues, "I want you to promise me you'll go rest as soon as I leave."

"I promise, Ma," Uncle Walt says.

"I'll be back later with beef stew for dinner tonight. That's still your favorite, isn't it?"

"It is, Ma," he tells her, though I know for a fact he eats more sushi these days than beef.

She kisses the top of his head, pulls herself up to her full height, which is maybe five feet, and leads Dad out the door.

"Wow," Uncle Walt says, "that did me in. Has she gotten confused like that before?"

"I don't think so," I say. "Not that I've noticed."

He nods, then grimaces as he hauls himself out of the chair. "Listen, guys, I do need to rest. Your room, right, Maze?"

"Yeah. I changed the sheets for you."

"Thanks, Hitchcock. You're the best." He ruffles my hair as he passes, and I don't mind one bit. I stand there with a bunch of dripping-wet rags in my hand and watch him go.

"He calls you Hitchcock," Hackett says softly. "You're lucky he's your uncle."

Oh, right. Hackett's still here. I take the rags out to the utility room and drop them in the deep sink. Cyrus and Hackett follow me.

"What should we do now?" Cyrus asks.

"We can go watch a movie at my house!" Hackett pipes up.

"I'm not watching *Blade Runner* again," I say.

"You've only seen it once," Cyrus says.

"Once was enough."

Hackett's face droops. "We could watch something else."

"Like what?"

He shrugs. "I've got *The Matrix* and all the *Star Wars* stuff."

I make a face. "I don't like movies where you're supposed to believe some dopey, mumbly guy gets it together long enough to save the world." Actually I really liked the *Star Wars* movie *The Force Awakens*, where the hero is a girl—it's just that being nice to Hackett feels like walking across hot coals.

There's a red flush creeping up Hackett's neck from under his collar. "Well, I don't have any *girl* movies!" he says.

I'm kind of surprised that Hackett can actually get mad about something. I'm pretty sure I've never seen that before. Still, he's not getting away with a crack like that.

"I don't watch *girl* movies!" I tell him. "I watch *great* movies! Movies you can believe in! Have you ever even seen *The Princess Bride*?"

He smirks. "You're saying *The Princess Bride* isn't a girl movie? Come on!"

Ha! He walked into my trap. *The Princess Bride* is one of Cyrus's favorites.

Cy's eyes bug out of their sockets. "Are you kidding, Gary? That movie's a classic!" He points an invisible sword at Hackett and says, "'My name is Inigo Montoya. You killed my father. Prepare to die.'"

Hackett looks confused. I can't believe he doesn't know the most famous line from one of the best movies of all time. It's sad, really. "Whatever," he says. "I'm going home. You two can watch princess movies without me." He bangs out through the back door. "I'll see you later, Cy, when *she's* not around."

Which makes me feel a little bad. I've never actually been so mean to Hackett that he's gotten mad at me. But all I say to Cy is, "Good. He's gone."

Cyrus starts running water in the kitchen sink so he can wash the empty soda and beer glasses. He likes to be helpful. "Gary's not that bad, Maisie. Why do you hate him so much? He's the only other movie geek we know."

I shrug. "He doesn't like the movies I like. Besides, he acts so dorky."

"Only when you're around. You make him nervous."

"*I* make him nervous? Why?"

"Because you're so hard on him."

"Well, he acts like he's our new best friend, and I don't like it. I already have a best friend." As soon as I say that, I feel a little nervous. Cyrus and I always said we were best friends when we were little kids, but it occurs to me we haven't said it much lately. Are we still best friends?

Some people think a boy and a girl can't be friends when they get to be our age, but I don't see why that should be true. Harry Potter was friends with Hermione without wanting to kiss her or anything. Veronica Mars was best friends with Wallace. Buffy never dated Xander, at least not in the four seasons I've watched. It's not like we invented the idea.

"Well, sure," Cy says easily. "We'll always be best friends, Maze, but that doesn't mean we can't have other friends too."

I'm so relieved that Cyrus is still my best friend, I feel a little less aggravated about Hackett. I get a dish towel and start drying the glasses while Cyrus moves on to scrubbing the lasagna pan Mom left soaking in the sink last night.

"I guess you're right," I say. "Okay. You can be friends with Hackett if you want to, as long as I don't have to spend too much time with him."

Cy scrubs a few more seconds and then stops and looks at me. "You don't get it, Maze."

"Don't get what?"

"It's not me that Gary really wants to hang around with. It's you."

The idea that Hackett wants to hang around with me is too bizarre to deal with, so I put it away in the deepest drawer of my mind, where I hope it will get lost forever. I have other things to think about right now. My end-of-the-year project for history class is to interview an older person about what New Aztec was like when they were growing up. I've already done one interview with Grandma—filmed it, in fact, with my video camera—but after what happened Sunday, I'm nervous about going back for a second. What if she tries to remember something and can't, and she starts crying again?

"She's fine," Mom assures me. "I'm sure it was just a momentary thing. We all forget stuff as we get older."

Uncle Walt is lying on the couch. I wonder if he's more worried than Mom is—she wasn't actually there when it happened—but he just winks and says, "May the Force be with you."

So after school I walk to Grandma's house. Cy doesn't come along because on Tuesdays he goes to a cartooning class at the library. Plus after what he told me Sunday afternoon, I'm a little bit embarrassed around him. We finished doing the dishes without saying one more word about Hackett, and then we went to Cy's house and watched, what else, *The Princess Bride*. But I couldn't even pay attention to the movie because my brain had stopped working. The gears were all gummed up thinking about Hackett and how and why and what comes next. I don't want *anything* to come next. I don't even want to see Hackett again! I've decided I'm just going to pretend Cyrus never told me anything.

Grandma is waiting for me at the kitchen table with a plate of homemade snickerdoodle cookies, and she seems fine, so I'm going with that. I can tell she's been out working in her tiny backyard garden because there's tracked-in mud on the kitchen floor and dirt under her fingernails. That seems like good news—nothing makes her happier than digging in dirt.

"So, what else do you want to know?" she asks

me, pushing the plate of cookies under my nose. "Last time we talked about what my grade school was like and what games we played and all that."

Phew, at least she remembers that much. I relax a little and take a cookie in one hand while I raise the video camera with the other. "Tell me about your parents. What did they do?"

She leans back in her chair. "Well, Mom and Dad owned a little market up on Lebanon Avenue. Where the vacuum cleaner place is now. You knew that."

"What did the store look like? How big was it?"

She looks out the window as if she can see into the old store. Her face gets kind of soft, and I zoom in for a close-up. It's funny, but looking at her through the lens is almost like looking back in time. For some reason I feel like I can see what she used to look like before she was a grandma—or even a mother. Very pretty and very lively, with a quick smile that lit up her face.

"The market was a small place and kind of dark inside. But they carried everything. My father was a butcher, so there was always fresh meat. My mother worked the cash register and did the bookkeeping. We got vegetables from the local farmers. Only what was in season, of course. You couldn't get asparagus and green beans year-round like you do now."

"Did you ever work in the store?"

"Oh, sure, when I was in high school. My friend Hank worked there too. He used to drive the delivery truck for Dad, but if there weren't any deliveries to make, he'd help me restock the shelves. It was always more fun when Hank was there. He had such a great sense of humor."

This is the first I've heard of anybody named Hank, but I need to get this interview done, so I try to get her back on track. "How was your store different from the supermarkets we shop in now?"

But Grandma is still staring off into space. "He was a few years older than me, but always so nice. I never meant to hurt his feelings. I was just so young and naive, I didn't even understand what was going on." She gives a little laugh. "Or maybe I was afraid to."

"You mean with Hank? What *was* going on?" I ask. I'm not sure this should be on film, so I turn the camera off and put it down.

"Oh, I guess he had a crush on me. I was very innocent for fifteen. I didn't understand that when a boy teases you like that and hangs around to talk to you when his shift is over, that means he likes you."

Huh. Was this something I had in common with Grandma? Apparently she'd been clueless about some boy liking her too. Well, how are you supposed to know unless they tell you? On the other hand, the idea of Hackett actually telling me, in *person*, makes me feel sick to my stomach.

I decide maybe I should get this on film. Even if I don't use it in the final video, it could be useful to me, so I turn on the camera again. "So, what happened to him? To Hank?" I ask.

"We stayed friends until I went off to college. Hank couldn't afford college, so he stayed here. But after I left, something bad happened to him. What was the story? Oh, yes! He'd been fishing in the Mill River up north, just below where the dam is. Some young boys, ten or twelve years old, were fooling around at the top of the falls, and one of them fell off the dam. Must have hit his head when he fell, because he didn't even try to swim out of the current. What I heard was Hank jumped in to save him. It was very rocky right there, and Hank hurt himself jumping in—broke his arm, I think—but he got to the boy anyway and pulled him out. But it was too late. They couldn't bring him around."

"The boy died?"

Grandma nodded. "I saw Hank when I was home from college on vacation, and it seemed like that changed him. Not being able to save that boy. Nobody could have, of course, but he felt it was his responsibility and he'd failed at it. It changed him, took away his jolly humor. If I remember correctly, he joined the navy soon after that."

It was a pretty awful story, but I was relieved that Grandma's memory was good enough to recall it. And I was also glad I'd kept on filming. I might be able to use some of it for my project.

"I guess Hank was in the navy for a while, and then he moved to New York City. I remember thinking that sounded like the end of the earth." Grandma looks down at her knobby fingers, examining them as if she's surprised at how they look. I focus the camera on her hands, wondering how it feels to have arthritis buckle your joints like that.

"Meanwhile," she continues, "I met your grandpa at Illinois State, and that was that. He seemed so smart to me, and we got along real well. I moved back here and taught school for a year or two, but I was ready to get married when he asked. I guess my life doesn't sound very exciting to you."

"So you never saw Hank again?"

"Sure, I saw him sometimes. After he moved back from New York, he bought the Lincoln Theater. Every time Grandpa and I went there, he gave me a free box of popcorn. Of course, he didn't like Grandpa much—they'd glare at each other like two boxers in the ring. When VCRs came out, and then DVD players, we stopped going to the theater and just watched movies at home so Grandpa didn't have to put up with Hank giving him the evil eye. I haven't seen Hank in years."

"I guess Hank must have sold the Lincoln Theater to Mr. Schmitz," I say.

Grandma laughs. "Maisie, Hank *is* Mr. Schmitz. Henry Schmitz. He still owns the place, as far as I know."

I'm so shocked, I put the camera down. Grumpy old Mr. Schmitz is Hank, who used to have a crush on my grandma? Who had a great sense of humor? Who jumped into a river to save a drowning kid?

"I used to love going to the Lincoln." Grandma is staring into space again. "The seats were red velvet, and the curtain that opened in front of the screen was gold. It was the most beautiful place in New Aztec."

I don't tell her that it doesn't look so great these days. There's not much red velvet left on those seats, and half of them are broken. There's no curtain over the screen either, and I doubt Mr. Schmitz has given out a free box of popcorn in this century. Still, knowing what I know now about him makes me like him a little more, or at least like the guy he used to be, Grandma's old friend.

"What were your favorite movies?" I ask her, picking up the camera again.

"Oh, I loved *The King and I* with Yul Brynner

and Deborah Kerr. When they waltzed together, my friends all swooned. And also *South Pacific*. I'd dance around my bedroom singing "I'm Gonna Wash That Man Right Outa My Hair." We saw all the musicals. And *Roman Holiday* with Gregory Peck and Audrey Hepburn. We all loved Audrey—she was small, but she had spunk. Oh, and *Cat on a Hot Tin Roof* with Paul Newman and Elizabeth Taylor. That was very racy for the times, and our mothers didn't want us to go, but we sneaked out and saw it anyway."

"I haven't seen any of those," I say.

"You can wait a few years for *Cat on a Hot Tin Roof*. My girlfriends and I used to go to the Lincoln every Saturday afternoon. In those days it only cost twenty-five cents."

"Cyrus and I go to the Lincoln Theater every Saturday too," I say. "It costs more than a quarter now, but it's still cheaper than movies at the mall. And we like the old films Mr. Schmitz gets."

"Well, you'll have to give my best to Hank next time you go. I think he'd remember me. Tell him Evelyn Hoffmeister from the market says hello."

Right. And then he'd give *me* the evil eye. Of course, he usually did that anyway.

Grandma stands up and gets an old, dented pot from the drawer under her stove. "Do you want some tea, sweetheart?"

"Sure."

She runs water into the pot.

"What happened to your teakettle?" I ask her.

"Oh . . ." She makes a brushing gesture with her hand, as if she wants to sweep my question away. "I had an accident."

"You dropped it?" Why would that hurt a metal teakettle?

She turns to face me. "Don't tell your mother. She'll worry, and it's not a big deal."

"I won't tell her." It's an easy promise to make, since I usually tell my mother as little as possible.

Grandma bites her bottom lip. "Last week I put some water on to boil and I forgot about it . . . and the kettle melted on the stove."

It *melted*? I get up and go over to the stove. My fingers brush the gray crust that surrounds one of the burners.

"I cleaned it up," Grandma says. "You can't really tell." Which isn't true.

"How long did you . . . forget about it?"

"Oh, not that long. I got busy with something else and . . . you know how it is. It slipped my mind."

I don't know what to say, so I don't say anything. I'm sure that kettle whistled. And there are only four small rooms in this place—she couldn't have been too far away. Did she leave it on when she went outside?

She fixes us cups of Earl Grey tea with lots of milk, the way I like it. I'm still thinking about how long it must take to melt a teakettle when she brings the cups to the table.

"You know what I just remembered?" she says. "I went to a dance with some girlfriends one night, at that lodge out on Raccoon Lake. Might have been a birthday party for someone. I was probably seventeen. Oh, I haven't thought about this in years!" A smile creeps over her face. I think about picking up the camera again, but I don't. It seems like Grandma is about to say something more personal than what I need for my project. "Hank was there, and we danced together a few times. There was a big porch on one end of the lodge that overlooked the lake, and we went out there by ourselves, Hank and I."

"After you . . . danced with him?" I try to picture my funny, forgetful grandma and old Mr. Schmitz dancing. Did they dance close together? Did he have his arms around her? I can't even imagine it.

She nods. "I think the party was almost over. We went out on that porch, and . . . and he kissed me."

"Mr. Schmitz *kissed* you?" I suddenly have an awful feeling that Grandma might be remembering things that didn't really happen.

She giggles in a way I'm not sure I've ever

heard before. "I kissed him back too. And then I ran away. Isn't that silly? I was such a scaredy-cat in those days. I guess I thought I'd done something terrible, kissing that older boy. I don't think I ever told a soul. Until today." She reaches over and pats my hand with her stiff fingers.

I smile and take a drink of my tea. I don't really want to be the keeper of Grandma's secrets. I'm not sure I even want to be the keeper of my *own* secrets, but I guess I don't have much choice.

"Let's film a movie scene and put it on YouTube," Cyrus says. "We haven't done that in a while."

"Okay," I agree. "Can we use your dad's tripod again?"

"Sure. We got a ton of hits on our *2001: A Space Odyssey* scene. You were so funny as HAL."

"Thank you, Dave," I say in my robot voice, and Cy laughs. "You were really good as Don Corleone in *The Godfather* too. That one was really popular."

"I love doing Marlon Brando."

It's Friday afternoon and pouring down rain, so Cyrus and I are in the basement at his house. His dad calls this the rec room, but the only recreation I've ever seen him do down here is watch TV. The washing machine and dryer are both rumbling in the corner, and Cy's mother comes down every twenty minutes or so to check on them, so there's not much privacy. Grandma's at our house, making another of Uncle Walt's favorite meals while Mom complains about the mess she's making, so it's noisy over there too.

Cy hasn't mentioned the thing about Hackett again all week, so I'm pretending it never happened. Maybe it didn't. Maybe I dreamed it. Or nightmared it.

"We could do a scene from *Back to the Future* or *The Breakfast Club*," Cy says.

I nod, but I'm thinking of older movies. "Or how about a Katharine Hepburn–Spencer Tracy movie, like *Adam's Rib* . . . or, no, I want to play Rosalind Russell in *His Girl Friday* in that scene where she calls the other reporter a double-crossing chimpanzee!"

"Then what's my part? The chimpanzee? Let's do *The Jerk*, and I can be Steve Martin."

"You always want to do Steve Martin movies, but then there's no good role for me," I complain.

"You can be the Bernadette Peters character," he says.

"Oh, right. The scene where she disco dances, or the one where she sings and plays the trumpet? I can't do any of that stuff. I want to say the funny lines."

"Well, it's hard to find a movie with two equally good roles," Cyrus says. "Unless it's, like, a love story or something." We sometimes watch love stories, but we never film scenes from them. That would be gross.

"Which is why we should just write our own movie and film it," I say.

Cyrus thinks it over. "That's a lot harder," he says.

"I know, but then it's really *our* movie, not just an imitation of somebody else's."

"Maybe we could make it a fantasy," he says. "It could start out with a grandmother reading a book to her grandson, and then suddenly the story becomes real, and—"

"That's how *The Princess Bride* starts." I pick up my camera and start filming Cy's cat, Edward Scissorhands, who's lying on his back on the corner of the desk and is just about to fall off. He's rolling over. Here it comes.

"No, it isn't," Cy says. "That was a grand*father*."

Ker-plop. The cat tips over the side of the desk, scratches madly at the air, eyes popping, then lands on the floor, feet first. He turns to lick his shoulder as if he hasn't just humiliated himself. Got it—that's going on my YouTube channel. I reach down to pet Edward, but he flounces away as if he's not the least bit embarrassed by his clumsiness.

I put down the camera. "Cy, our movie has to

be something brand-new that nobody's ever seen before."

"Is that even possible?" he asks.

"I don't know, but I think we should try for it."

"Well, there have to be two kids in it, a boy and a girl, so we can both be main characters," Cyrus says. "Or we could get somebody else to do it with us. Like—"

"No!" I cut him off before he can suggest the person I know he's about to. "Just the two of us."

"Maisie, what kind of a movie has only two people in it? I was thinking Gary might want to—"

"I knew you were going to say *him*!" I bang my fist on the desk, and the can of pens leaps into the air. "Why do we have to include him in everything now?"

Cy stares at the blank computer screen. "We don't *have* to. I just thought he'd like to do it with us."

Neither of us speaks for a minute, and then I say, "You know what? If we need another person in the movie, maybe it should be an adult. Uncle Walt could do it. I mean, he's a *real* actor."

Cy nods his head slowly. "True. But he's not in great shape right now. We'd have to explain why he's all banged up."

I think this over. "Okay, I've got it," I say. "One of us is a ghost and is haunting the other person.

Uncle Walt is the father of the ghost. He was driving the car that killed the ghost kid, which is why he's hurt too."

Cy's eyebrows go up. "I like the ghost idea. If the father is injured, the accident must have just happened."

"Right. Maybe we can have a funeral for the ghost kid, and that's the first time the other kid sees her."

"*Her*? You mean you're the ghost kid? I want to be the ghost."

"My skin is a lot paler than yours. I look more like a ghost."

"So? Ever heard of makeup?"

"It's my idea," I say.

"But the ghost is the best role. You always want the best role."

"Well, sure I do. So do you!"

Cyrus sighs loudly. "What does the other kid do? Just scream and run away?"

"No, he . . ." What does he do? "He helps the ghost kid tell her father not to feel so bad because she's happy being dead."

"What's so good about being dead?"

"You can scare people, right? That would be fun."

Cyrus's mother bustles down the stairs, carrying a laundry basket. "What on earth are you two talking about? There's nothing good about being dead! Don't even say that!" She drops the laundry basket and flies over to us with her hand over her heart.

"We're writing a screenplay, Mom," Cy explains. "About a ghost kid who was killed in a car accident."

"Oh, Cyrus!" She closes her eyes and shakes her head back and forth. "No, no, no. You are *not* writing about that! It's bad luck! I forbid it! There are much nicer things you can write about that don't tempt fate."

"But, Mom—"

"Absolutely not!" She starts to walk away, then turns back. "Why don't you write about two kids who . . . find a treasure chest in their backyard?"

We smile at her until she bends over to take the clothes out of the dryer, then we look at each other and roll our eyes. A treasure chest. Yeah, that's never been done before.

"Or how about this," she says. "Write about two kids who help their mother fold the laundry, after which she makes them strawberry smoothies."

Mrs. Hapsburger is no dummy. She knows we love her strawberry smoothies.

"Whenever you're ready," she calls as she hauls the basket upstairs. "I've got that vanilla yogurt you like."

"Okay, Mom. In a few minutes," Cy says.

"We're not really giving up our idea, are we?" I ask him. "It's good. Everybody likes ghost stories."

"I know," he says, "but maybe she's right about tempting fate. I mean, what if one of us *did* get in a car accident? Wouldn't you feel bad?"

"That isn't going to happen. You just don't want me to be the ghost."

"Well, I don't see why you always get the good part. When we made the vampire video, you got to be the vampire, and I had to be the one who got bitten!"

"I thought you *wanted* to be the dead kid," I say.

"The dead kid wasn't the best part in that one!"

I sigh. Yes, all right, I do like to have the best part. Well, who doesn't? Being a ghost would be so much fun!

"Okay. I guess we could both be ghosts," I say. But obviously we need to have somebody be the person who gets scared by the ghosts, because that's how you get the audience to believe in them. And I know who Cyrus will want to play that part.

Cy turns off the computer. "Let's take a break. I want a smoothie."

We trudge to the stairs. "I'm not going to fold underwear, though," I tell him.

"Okay," he says. "You can do the T-shirts."

"Deal." We high-five and go upstairs to find his mother.

Uncle Walt is lying on the living room couch with a pillow propping up one shoulder. "Aw, man, I'd like to go with you guys, but I can't sit in a hard chair that long."

"But it's *Psycho*," I say. "How often do you get to see Hitchcock's best movie on a big screen?"

Uncle Walt squints one eye. "*Best*? That's debatable, Hitch. What about *The Birds*, or *Vertigo*? Those are right up there too."

"Okay," I say, "but *Psycho* is the first American movie to show a toilet on-screen. You have to admit that makes it historically cool."

Uncle Walt laughs, but he's not really looking at me anymore. He's got his laptop open, probably scanning through the *Hollywood Reporter* site or other websites that list upcoming auditions, like he does every morning.

"Are you looking for another job?" I ask.

"Just keeping up to date. My agent will let me know if there's something she thinks I should go up for. Of course, I can't really audition for anything in this condition, but I want to keep up with what's happening out there."

"You need to get another big movie."

"Yeah. Easier said than done. Most of the ads this morning are for stupid commercials and student films. Or, listen to this one: 'Casting an original TV pilot script called *Treading Water*, about an Olympic swimmer who falls in love with the oddball she rescues from drowning.' That's got 'canceled after two episodes' written all over it."

"If it even gets picked up at all," I say. Uncle Walt explained to me once that a lot of pilot episodes get produced, but the networks and cable channels only pick up a handful of shows to become actual TV series.

"Oh, it's just dumb enough to get picked up." Uncle Walt sighs. "Maybe your mother's right. I should give up on acting and get a real job." But he looks up at me and grins. "Nah!"

"Mom's just jealous because she's stuck here in New Aztec while you're out in LA having fun," I say. "You're bound to get your big break soon."

"We'll see. You'd better go collect Cyrus if you don't want to be late for the movie."

I head for the door. I will not let Uncle Walt give up on his dreams!

He calls after me. "The creepiest moment in *Psycho* is when Norman tells Marion that a boy's best friend is his mother. Watch Tony Perkins's face in that scene—it goes from sweet and vulnerable to what-the-heck-is-going-on-in-that-mind, and then back to innocence. You can read the character's whole life on Tony's face. Fabulous performance."

I smile. He won't give up acting.

★★

Cyrus is just wheeling his bike out of the garage when I bring mine around front. We ride to the Lincoln without talking much, which is not that unusual, but after what he told me last weekend about Hackett, our not-talking seems louder than it ought to be.

As we're locking our bikes to the parking meter, I see a familiar figure walking toward us from the bus stop. I hit Cy on the arm to make him look up.

"Oh, yeah," he says. "I forgot to tell you. Gary wanted to come too."

"What do you mean, you *forgot* to tell me?" I hiss at him. "Now our Saturday is ruined. What am I supposed to *do*?"

"What do you mean? You don't have to *do* anything. Just sit there and watch the movie."

"Well, he's sitting by you, not me!"

Cy doesn't have time to answer because Hackett's right there already. He's wearing shorts, which make his legs look really long. You can tell he plays soccer, because his calf muscles are—ugh! Why am I looking at his legs?

I say, "Hey," really fast and head for the box office. Kathy, who sits in the little booth every Saturday afternoon, takes my five dollars and gives me my ticket as if she's never seen me before. While the boys are getting their tickets, I head inside.

As soon as I see Mr. Schmitz at the concession stand, I remember Grandma's stories about him. It's hard to imagine him dancing with anybody, much less kissing them. Blech. I guess I'm staring at him a little bit. He looks up and says, "Whaddaya want?"

"Um, popcorn, I guess. Small."

He turns around and grabs a red-and-white box from a stack. The popcorn machine whirs, throwing up yellowish white kernels that Mr. Schmitz shovels into the box with a scoop.

"My grandma says she knows you," I tell him. "She said I should say hi to you from her."

By now Cy and Hackett have come inside too.

They're standing next to me, looking into the candy case.

Mr. Schmitz turns around and bangs the pop-corn box down on the counter so a few pieces jump out. He grunts. "I guess I know a lot of people's grandmas and grandpas. What's the name?"

"Evelyn. Evelyn Hoffmeister. You used to work at her parents' grocery store on Lebanon Avenue."

Mr. Schmitz's face goes slack, and his mouth falls open like he's just been hit over the head. It reminds me of what Uncle Walt said about Tony Perkins, about how you could read the character's whole life on his face. Mr. Schmitz's eyes go out of focus for a minute, and then he says, quietly, "Evie."

"Oh, yeah, people used to call her Evie."

"I haven't seen her in years," he says, looking at me now. "How is she?"

"She's fine."

"Doesn't go to the movies anymore, I guess."

"My grandpa liked to watch DVDs," I said. "But he died a few years ago."

"He did?" Mr. Schmitz asks. "I didn't see that in the paper."

"Grandma didn't put it in. She doesn't like obituaries. She says they're half bragging and half crying, and it's not a good combination."

He grunts. "That sounds like Evie. She still live in that house on Jefferson?"

"No, she moved to a condo last year. Over on Bristow Street."

Mr. Schmitz slowly shakes his head. "Evie Hoffmeister."

I put my two dollars on the counter, but Mr. Schmitz waves them away. "No charge," he says. "You're a good customer."

I stand over to the side while Cy and Hackett get their popcorn. Mr. Schmitz makes them pay even though they're good customers too. It's Grandma. I got her free popcorn.

★8★

I hate walking my bike when I could be riding it. It's hot and muggy, and it would feel good to have a breeze blowing over me. But Hackett walked to the movie, and now he wants to come back to Cy's house with us (or that's what he *says*), so we walk our bikes the whole way home. It makes the trip twice as long. Or maybe it just seems long because I'm so twitchy and uncomfortable around Hackett now.

Maybe Cyrus is wrong about Hackett hanging around us because he likes me. That's what he meant, right? That Hackett likes me *that* way. Of all the possible boys, why *him*? I mean, he's nice-looking, I guess, if you don't mind that his hair is always hanging in his face, and he's not one of those jerky guys who try to be funny by insulting people, but he's still a *boy*. I guess when I think about it, Hackett is actually one of the better boys.

It's just that I don't want *anybody* to like me like that. I'm not usually afraid of stuff, but in this one way, I guess I'm a little like my grandma—I'm kind of scared about boys.

The thing is, if a boy likes you and then you like him back, everything starts to change. I've seen it happen to other girls—one day they're regular twelve-year-olds, and the next day they're giggling and squealing and acting like their brains have leaked out of their ears.

Cy and Hackett are walking a little bit ahead of me, but I can still hear them.

"Man, that shower scene is scary, even when you know it's coming," Hackett says.

"Yeah," Cyrus says. "I read that Janet Leigh was afraid to take showers after she saw herself in the movie."

"No kidding. I think *I'm* afraid to take showers now too," Hackett says. He turns around and looks at me. "I can see why it's your favorite movie, though. I liked it a lot."

"It's not my favorite movie," I say. "It's my favorite Hitchcock movie."

He nods. "I haven't seen any others, so I guess it's my favorite too."

"You should see *The Birds* and *Vertigo* before you decide," I tell him. "Those are my uncle's favorites."

"Okay!" Hackett seems ridiculously happy, like I just gave him a puppy. "Maybe they'll come to the Lincoln, and we can go see them together!"

Ugh, I didn't mean *that*. But against my will, my mouth seems to be curving up at one corner. He looks so pleased, it's hard not to be happy along with him. I wish he was wearing long pants.

"You know, it took a week to shoot that shower scene," Cyrus says. "They used fifty different camera angles."

I correct him. "Seventy-seven camera angles. There were fifty cuts—that's probably what you're thinking of."

"Oh, right."

"What do you mean, cuts?" Hackett asks me.

"You know, in the editing. There are fifty cuts in that one three-minute scene. You see it in quick pieces instead of one long shot, which makes it more frightening. That's the genius of Hitchcock."

Hackett has dropped back so he's walking with me now, behind Cy. He leans in a little bit too closely. "How come you know so much about movies?"

"Because I want to. Because I read about them. I love movies . . . and so does Cyrus. Right, Cy?" As I'm talking I manage to speed up so I'm walking next to Cyrus, and Hackett is following behind us. Yes, this is much better. Hackett makes me nervous. I take a deep breath and sneak a look at Cy.

He's staring down at the sidewalk like he's searching for loose change.

By the time we get back to our neighborhood, I'm exhausted trying to figure out what to say to Hackett and how to act around him. The boys turn in to Cy's driveway, but I have to get away.

"I'm gonna head home," I say. "I told Uncle Walt I'd help him . . . do some laundry." Weak excuse, but I started the sentence before I knew how it was going to end.

"Can't he do it himself?" Hackett asks. He looks disappointed. "He can still use one of his arms."

"He gets tired out fast." I shrug. When you're lying, it's better not to give too many details that the listener can pick apart.

"Maybe I'll see you tomorrow," Hackett says.

God, he doesn't give up! I try to catch Cyrus's eye, but he's not looking at me. "I'm not sure what I'm doing tomorrow," I say, "but I'll probably see you at school on Monday." And then I drop my bike and dash into the house before he can come up with some plan for hanging out on Monday. What did I ever do to Hackett to make him like me? And how can I get him to *stop*?

I'm hoping to get a few minutes alone with Uncle Walt, but the whole family is home, all of them out in the backyard. Grandma always comes over for dinner on Saturday night, but I'll bet she spent most of the day at our house today because of Uncle Walt being here. I can tell Mom has been dealing with Grandma for at least a few hours because Mom has a hard look in her eyes that says, *Don't bug me, Maisie. I'm at the end of my rope already.*

Dad is pushing the lawn mower up and down the yard, and whenever he gets close to the patio you can't hear anything but the angry whine of the engine as the mower chews up grass. I swing my video camera up and get some footage of him breathing heavily as he passes by. His sweaty scowl says, *I'd rather be bowling.* Mom is filling the patio pots with potting soil and geraniums, and I get her wiping a muddy glove across her forehead so it's streaked with dirt. She glares into the camera and draws a finger across her throat. Cut.

Instead I turn the camera in the other direction. Grandma is perching on a chair next to Uncle Walt, who's sprawled on a chaise lounge. His head is back, a baseball cap pulled low over his eyes, and his arm on the broken side rests on a pillow. I get an interesting two-shot of them that I think I might even be able to use in my history project video.

"Come sit down, Cindy," Grandma says in her insistent voice, the one she uses with Mom but seldom with anybody else. "It's your day off."

"I want to get these planted, Ma. If I don't do it on my 'day off,' when will it get done?"

"Weekends are for resting!" Grandma says, as if Mom was breaking some law by planting flowers on a Saturday.

Mom smears another swish of dirt on her face. "I don't want to rest. I want to accomplish something. Besides, when did you ever rest when we were kids?"

Uncle Walt laughs. "She's got you there, Ma. You never sat still. Pop used to say you were on springs. He'd try to make you sit down, but you'd bounce right back up again."

Grandma ignores him and turns to me. "Maisie,

come and talk to me. What have you been up to this afternoon?" She pats the chair next to her, and I lower the camera and sit down.

"I went to the movies with Cy."

"You two are quite the couple, aren't you?" she says, smiling. I'm not sure what she means by that. Cy and I are certainly not "a couple." Unless she means a couple of friends.

"How was *Psycho*?" Uncle Walt asks.

"Great. But I knew it would be."

"*Psycho*?" Grandma turns wide eyes on me. "That terrifying Alfred Hitchcock movie? You're much too young to see that!"

"Grandma, I've seen it three times already. The shower scene is the only scary part."

"As I recall, the ending is terrifying! Oh, that movie gave me nightmares."

"By the way, I told Mr. Schmitz you said hello. He remembered you right away. He asked me where you lived."

"He did? Really? Isn't that sweet." She gets a faraway look in her eyes and folds her hands carefully in her lap.

"Who's Mr. Schmitz?" Mom wants to know. "You mean that old guy who runs the Lincoln?"

I nod. "He used to have a crush on Grandma."

"What?" Uncle Walt sits up straight and removes the baseball cap. "I never heard that story!"

"Neither have I," Mom says. "You dated that guy before you met Pop?"

"Oh, I never dated him. There's no story," says Grandma, although I know better. "We were kids. He worked at your granddad's store. He was a nice boy."

"He's an old grouch now," Mom says. "Last time I went there, he bit my head off because I didn't have exact change for a bag of M&M's."

"Well, life can make you that way, I guess," Grandma says. "He was very kind to me in the old days."

"He gave me free popcorn today," I said. "Just like he used to give you."

Grandma smiles, but she looks kind of sad too. She pushes out of her chair and stands up. "I'm going inside to get some lemonade. Can I bring anybody anything?"

"I'll have some too, if you can carry it," Mom says.

"Of course I can carry it." Grandma sounds insulted. "Anybody else?"

"Sure," Uncle Walt says.

"I'll help you, Grandma," I say, and I get up to go with her. I get a little sidetracked when I see Cy and Hackett walking down the street, so I sneak to the side of the house to watch them. I wonder where they're going, and why they didn't ask me to go along. Not that I want to hang out with them. I mean, I'd want to hang with Cy if Hackett wasn't always with him now.

When I get to the kitchen, Grandma is standing in front of the open refrigerator, staring at the gallon milk jug as if she expects it to speak to her.

"I can't remember what I came in here for," she says. "Walter wanted something, didn't he?"

"Lemonade, remember? Everybody wants lemonade."

She turns and gives me a grateful look. "Thank you, Cindy. Lemonade for you and your brother."

My smile freezes on my face.

Grandma gets out the pitcher of lemonade and stirs it up while I put five glasses on a tray. Forgetting Grandpa was dead, melting her teakettle, and now thinking that I'm my mother. Three weird things in a week. Should I tell Mom?

I pick up the tray of glasses and push open the screen door, holding it for Grandma to follow with the pitcher.

"Thank you, Maisie," she says. "You're my favorite grandchild, even if you are the only one."

I take a deep breath. Okay, Grandma's back again. I don't have to tell Mom. I don't have to break my promise. I don't have to think about what it means that sometimes Grandma can't remember who I am.

I call Cyrus the minute I see his parents' car turn in to the driveway after church. We don't go to church much anymore because Dad doesn't like the minister, who he says is so arrogant he acts like he brought the tablets down from the mountaintop himself. And Mom can't stand the organist, who has no sense of rhythm.

"You didn't make plans with Hackett today, did you?" I ask Cy.

"Not really," he says. "I mean, I said maybe we could get together."

"Well, tell him you can't. Say you have to do something with your family."

"You mean, *lie* to him?"

"Please, Cyrus! I know you don't like to lie, but just this once. I really need to talk to you. *Alone*."

"I'm not a good liar, Maisie. You know that. What if he figures it out?"

"He won't. A lot of people get roped into family stuff on Sundays."

"Okay." He sighs deeply, as if I'm asking him to rob an old lady or something. Cyrus really is the kindest person I know. He never lies, he's never mean, and if I needed a kidney or just about anything else he has two of, I know he'd give me one. But sometimes I wish he could be just a little bit less perfect. (He probably wishes I could be a little bit *more* perfect, but I don't see that happening.)

He comes over as soon as he finishes lunch. I'm sitting at the picnic table in our backyard, looking at my favorite book, *Cinematic Storytelling*, but I have to read lines over and over because I'm too distracted to concentrate. Cyrus has a DVD in his hand.

"What did you bring?"

"*Napoleon Dynamite*. I thought after *Psycho* we needed a laugh."

I nod. "Okay. But later. First we have to talk."

"About Gary?"

Ugh. I feel a little nauseated now. "That too, but something else first. You know how last weekend my grandma forgot my grandpa was dead? Two more crazy things like that happened this week. She doesn't want me to tell Mom about it, but I don't know. Do you think I should?"

Cy doesn't say anything, but he stares at his hands for a long time. I pass the time picking the dead leaves off Mom's new geranium plants, which already look a little droopy. Finally I can't wait anymore. "Well, what do you *think*?"

"I'm trying to remember this movie I saw a while ago about a woman who had Alzheimer's. Her husband put her in a home for—"

"Cy, this isn't a movie—it's real! And I don't want my grandma to get stuck away in some horrible nursing-home place."

He looks back down at his hands. "I don't think they're all horrible. In this movie—"

"Forget about the movie and tell me what to do!"

He sighs. "Well, I guess I think keeping a secret is sort of like lying. It doesn't seem as bad, but it kind of is. Especially if it's about something important."

I knew he'd say that. "But maybe I'm wrong. Everybody forgets things sometimes. And now that I think about it, Grandma remembered all these movies she'd seen when she was really young, so maybe she's fine. If I tell my mother and she freaks out and puts Grandma in one of those places, it'll be my fault. I don't know. I think I should wait and see."

Cyrus shrugs. "You know your grandma better

than I do. But you asked me, Maze, so you must be a little worried."

One thing is for sure: nobody knows me better than Cy. "I am, a little. But maybe I'm just worrying for nothing." I thought of Grandma telling me about her father's store and about dancing with Mr. Schmitz. And that awful story about Mr. Schmitz trying to save the drowning kid. If she could remember all that stuff that happened a million years ago, she must be okay. Right?

"So, wanna go watch the movie?" Cy asks.

"In a minute."

I stand up and walk to the edge of the patio, where the grass clippings from the lawn mower decorate the concrete slab. I try to brush them off with the sole of my sneaker, but it only makes a green smear.

"You're freaked out about Gary, aren't you?" Cy asks me.

"I'm not 'freaked out.' I just . . . I don't *want* Hackett to like me. Is that so terrible?"

"I think you should start calling him Gary," Cy says. "If somebody likes you, you shouldn't call him by his last name."

"Oh, come on, Cyrus. I like calling him Hackett. It's the sound a cat makes when it throws up hair balls."

Cy gives me a disgusted nose-wrinkle. "Why

are you making such a big deal out of this, Maisie? He just *likes* you. Why is that so hard to put up with? He's a nice guy!"

"He doesn't 'just' like me. He *like* likes me, right?"

"So what? It's a compliment."

"But I don't like him back. I don't like *anybody*."

"Thanks a lot."

"You know what I mean. *Like* like. It's . . . weird to start feeling all that stuff. Don't you think? You don't have a crush on anybody yet, do you?"

It looks like Cyrus is going to say something, but then he clamps his mouth shut and turns away from me.

"You don't, do you?" I ask him again. "I mean, you'd tell me if you did, right?"

Without answering me, Cy wanders off toward my mom's flowering cherry tree. He stands there, unconsciously pulling off petals. Mom would pin him to the clothesline if she saw him doing that, but fortunately she's at the grocery store.

I come up behind him. "You *would* tell me, wouldn't you?"

"Maze," he says quietly, "I can't tell you everything."

"What do you mean? Of course you can! You always tell me everything."

His face relaxes into a smile. "Well, I tell you most things."

"What *can't* you tell me?"

"Well, I can't tell you what I can't tell you, can I?" He acts like he's just teasing me, but something's wrong. His voice sounds kind of shaky. Surely, he can't . . . he doesn't like me *too*, does he? No, I'd know it, wouldn't I? I'd feel it, the way I felt it when Hackett (or Gary, or whatever) walked next to me and gave me that hopeless smile.

"Cyrus, come on! Tell me what you mean. You're the one who said a secret is almost as bad as a lie. If you don't tell me, you're lying to me."

"I know that, Maze. And I'm sorry. I'm really sorry."

Oh my God, there are *tears* in his eyes. Honest-to-God tears! But he blinks them back and gives a little laugh.

"You know what?" he says. "I'm gonna go on home. You can keep *Napoleon Dynamite*. I'll get it from you later."

"Cyrus, wait a minute!" I yell after him, but he runs out of my yard and disappears. Maybe Gary Hackett is a better friend to Cyrus than I am. I almost made him cry, and I don't even know why.

I stumble inside, trying to figure out what just happened, but I'm distracted by the loud, pleading voice coming from the living room. Uncle Walt is on the phone. He sounds frustrated, so I figure he's talking to his agent again.

"Yeah, I know, Francine, but what am I supposed to do? I can't lift anything heavier than a fork for another five weeks. I'm just sitting around here getting rusty. There aren't any acting classes or improv groups within fifty miles. I'm going stir-crazy!"

He sees me leaning in the doorway and waves me into a chair, but he's paying more attention to the woman on the phone than me.

"If I just knew I had an audition lined up for when I get back—or maybe I could read for that pilot over Skype!"

I sling my legs over the side of the big, cushy chair, something that Mom does not approve of, except, *why*? Am I hurting the chair?

"Stars do Skype auditions all the time," Uncle Walt says. "Benedict Cumberbatch did one for that picture he was in last—I *know* I'm not Benedict Cumberbatch, Francine. I'm just *saying*."

I'd really like some ice cream. When you're confused and sad, ice cream is like a promise that things will get better, but I know we don't have any, because I finished up the last frosty bites of chocolate chip a few days ago.

Uncle Walt is pacing back and forth in front of my chair. "Okay, okay. I'm *trying* not to worry. But see if you can line something up, okay? Can I call you tomorrow? Okay, later in the week. But don't forget, Francine. If you don't call me, I'm calling you."

He clicks off and flops onto the couch, then winces. "Damn, I keep forgetting I'm injured."

"I wish you could drive," I say.

"I wish I could drive too. I wish I could do a lot of things." He sounds as miserable as I feel.

"Can you walk?" I ask him.

"Of course I can walk. I didn't hurt my legs."

"I mean, could you walk, say, half a mile? We could go to Dairy Heaven on Route 17 for chocolate shakes."

He holds out his good arm. "Help me up. I am in dire need of a chocolate shake."

I scribble a note for Mom so she doesn't freak out when she gets back and nobody's home. We lock the front door and walk down the sidewalk. I can't stop myself from glancing up at Cy's bedroom window.

"You think Cyrus wants to come with us?" Uncle Walt asks.

"No. He's kind of . . . busy."

Uncle Walt nods. "Everybody's busy except me." He looks down at me. "Sorry, Hitch. I'm afraid I'm lousy company today."

I shrug. "It's okay. I kind of am too."

"There's a pilot in the works that I'd be perfect for. I *know* it. But they're going to audition people before I get back. I probably should have just stayed in LA and paid somebody to drive me around and do my shopping and cooking and stuff. Not that I can afford that, but I'm missing everything. Not to mention, the longer I stay here, the more I annoy your mother."

"No, you don't!" Obviously I'm a better liar than Cyrus. Mom is pretty much always annoyed with Uncle Walt, and this visit it seems worse than usual. "What's the show about?" I ask.

"It's a drama set in an art museum where several big paintings have just been stolen. Not the usual hospital or law firm setup."

"It would be so cool if you got on a TV show!"

"Yeah." Uncle Walt works up an optimistic smile. A tossed-out soda can is lying on the sidewalk, and he gives it a careless kick. It flips over the curb and lands in the street. If Dad was with us, he'd pick it up and carry it all the way home to the recycle bin. He even does that on his mail route sometimes.

"I'd actually be making a few bucks for a change," Uncle Walt says. "And the exposure you get on TV is amazing."

"It'd be your big break!" I almost back up and go get that can, but I don't want to point out that Uncle Walt *didn't* do it.

"Enough talk about my sorry career," he says. "What's going on with you? Did you love *Psycho* as much the third time through?"

"Oh, sure. I mean, the lighting's amazing!"

He laughs. "I love that lighting makes you swoon. If you don't turn out to be a director, you'll certainly be a DP."

Which means director of photography. Which would be a cool job too. But it's not *Psycho* I want to talk about right now.

"Uncle Walt, when did you start, you know, *liking* people?"

"What do you mean? I've always liked people. Most people, anyway."

"No, I mean—"

He stops walking for a minute. "Oh, you mean when did I start liking girls. Having crushes, that kind of thing."

I can feel my face getting red, but there's nobody else I can ask about this kind of stuff, and I need some advice. "Yeah, that kind of thing."

He's walking a little more slowly now, thinking. "The first person I crushed on was probably Emily Katz. I was in middle school, and she was a year older than me. We rode the bus to school together, and I always tried to sit in back of her so I could watch her long black hair swing around when she moved her head. Finally I got up the nerve to talk to her, but it didn't go well. I think she had a boyfriend already, and I was just some lowly sixth grader whose mother still picked out his clothes in the morning." He laughs. "I haven't thought about that in years."

"I guess she was pretty," I say.

"To tell you the truth, I can't remember what she looked like. I think I just liked her hair."

"I don't get why hair is such a big deal," I say.

"Search me, Hitch. All I can tell you is hormones like hair."

"So who was next? Who did you go out with first?"

He smiles. "In high school I fell for Stacy Carmichael. *Her* I remember! We only went out for a few weeks, but if you'd asked me then, I would have said those weeks were the high point of my life."

I'm not sure how much I want to know about Stacy Carmichael, but Uncle Walt doesn't go into any more details. "Is that what's going on with you these days? You got a crush on somebody? Not Cyrus, is it?"

"No! Cy and I aren't like that. We're best friends." At least I hope we still are.

Uncle Walt nods. "Okay."

"But I guess somebody has a crush on me, and I just . . . I don't really want him to."

"Ahh. Gary Hackett, maybe?"

Now I stop walking. "How did you know?"

"Just a guess. I saw him looking at you the other day, and I wondered."

How humiliating! People could tell! "I don't want him to like me! I don't know what to say to him or how to act. How do I make him stop?"

Uncle Walt puts his hand on my shoulder. "You can't *make* him stop, Maze. I mean, you could be mean to him, I guess—but it looks like you've already tried that approach and it didn't work. Sometimes it backfires, and the person just likes you more."

"*Why*? I wouldn't like somebody who was mean to me!"

He shrugs. "Sometimes you want what you can't have. But it's not like you to be mean, Hitch. I think it would be better to just talk to him."

"I can't! It's too embarrassing. What would I say?"

"Well, I think you should stay as close to the truth as possible without breaking the guy's heart."

Breaking his heart? The mere idea stuns me. Surely I don't have that much power, do I?

We've reached Dairy Heaven by now, so we stop talking to place our orders. "Two chocolate shakes with mint chip ice cream," Uncle Walt tells the guy at the window. That's what we always get, Uncle Walt and me.

We don't talk while the guy is scooping and drizzling and whirring the blender. My mouth waters, and I'm kind of hoping Uncle Walt will just forget what we were talking about so I can enjoy my shake. How can he help me, anyway? I'm sure he was never in such a stupid situation.

But when we park ourselves at a picnic table, he starts in right where we left off.

"Gary seems like a nice kid. What is it you don't like about him?"

It's a hard question to answer. "It's not that I don't like him. At first I was just mad that he was getting in between me and Cyrus. I thought he wanted to be Cy's new best friend and push me out of the way. But then Cy told me it's *me* Hackett wants to hang around with, and I think he's right because yesterday Hackett tried to walk next to me on the way home from the movie."

Uncle Walt smiles and drops a spoonful of ice cream on his shirt. He hasn't quite mastered getting food to his mouth with his left hand yet. "Sounds like he likes you," he says as he wipes at the spill with a napkin.

"*I know*! But I'm not trying to make him like me. I don't wear tight clothes or let my belly button hang out like some girls do. I'd feel creepy dressing like that."

"I'm glad to hear it," Uncle Walt says. "Which means Gary likes you for yourself and not for how sexy you look."

The word "sexy" makes me just about pass out. How can people talk about that stuff so easily? Like it's normal. The whole idea makes me so nervous that I start to sweat. "What should I do?" I ask Uncle Walt.

"Well, you could try to relax and enjoy it."

I shake my head. "I don't know how to enjoy it. It's . . . scary."

Uncle Walt thinks about that for a few minutes while he slurps up more of his shake. "I get that. New experiences can be scary. But, you know, a boyfriend is just a boy who's a friend, right?"

"No. Cyrus is a boy who's a friend. A boyfriend is somebody who thinks he can, I don't know, touch you and kiss you. I'm not ready for that stuff!" I can feel my hot face radiating embarrassment.

Uncle Walt puts down his spoon and looks serious. "You know, Hitch, the boy isn't the only one who makes those decisions. I mean, he shouldn't touch you or kiss you until you want him to do those things."

"But what if I *never* want him to do those things?"

"Well, then he'll just be your friend and not your boyfriend. But, Maisie, sooner or later you'll want somebody to do those things. It might not be Gary Hackett, but it'll be somebody."

"Are you sure?"

"I'm pretty sure." He turns back to his shake, and I start to slurp up mine too. "And here's one more thing for you to think about." He points his spoon at me.

"What?"

"Gary Hackett is probably just as scared as you are."

★77★

In order to stop thinking so much about the Gary Hackett problem, I start working on a screenplay of my own, which I'm calling *Arnold and Fawn*. It's kind of a takeoff on one of my favorite movies, *Harold and Maude*. I watch it again for the two-hundredth time to remind myself how extremely amazing it is. I mean, you wouldn't think a movie where (spoiler alert) one main character fakes his suicide and the other one kills herself would be so entertaining.

In my version I want Arnold to be older than Fawn, but then I wonder if it's creepy to have an old guy hanging around with a young girl, so I decide Arnold should be a dog instead. An old talking dog. Assuming I can't find a talking dog, the animal's speech would have to be in voice-over. The bigger problem is, where do I get a dog who can act?

The first scene opens with Fawn seeing Arnold sitting outside a grocery store. As she walks past him, he says:

ARNOLD
You look like someone I can trust.

Fawn is shocked and jumps back.

FAWN
Did you just . . . say something?

ARNOLD
Did you hear me say something?

FAWN
I . . . I thought I did.

ARNOLD
Well then, I must have said something.

FAWN
Wow. Does your owner know you can talk?

Arnold gives her a scathing look.

ARNOLD

I don't have an "owner."

FAWN

You don't?

ARNOLD

I used to, but he left me in the
garage all day long. By myself!
What kind of life is that for a
distinguished animal like me?
There was no one to talk to!

FAWN

So you ran away?

ARNOLD

I certainly did.

FAWN

Oh, you're so lucky! I want to run
away too! My owners—I mean, my
parents—are so boring.

ARNOLD

What's stopping you? You've got
four good legs. Well, two anyway.

By the end of the first scene, Fawn realizes how much she has in common with Arnold. Neither of them likes being penned up or having people boss them around. So Arnold and Fawn decide to run away together, and they get bus tickets to California. Of course, filming a dog on a cross-country bus trip will be difficult too, but when you're in the grip of a good idea, you can't let yourself get sidetracked by practical worries.

I start writing Sunday night after dinner. Mom sticks her head in the door of the den around ten o'clock and tells me to go to bed as soon as I finish my homework. I don't tell her I'm not doing homework. It's after midnight when I realize my eyes are drooping and the words are swimming around on the page, but even after I turn out the light and go to bed, I keep thinking about my script.

I wake up late and exhausted the next morning, so Mom offers to drive Cyrus and me to school. I close my eyes and lean my head against the window the whole way. If I wasn't so tired, I'd probably feel a little embarrassed about our talk yesterday, but now I'm having a hard time remembering what was weird about it.

"Why are you so tired?" Cy asks when we get out at school.

"I stayed up late writing a screenplay," I say.

"Really?" Cy looks excited, which is cool because

I'm pretty sure nobody else on earth will care one way or the other. "What's it about?"

I yawn and try to focus my brain. "The main character is a girl named Fawn, and she's kind of a cross between Ferris Bueller from *Ferris Bueller's Day Off* and Harold from *Harold and Maude*."

Cy looks confused. "Those characters aren't much alike, are they?" he asks.

"Sure they are. They're both trying to figure out how to make their boring lives fun."

Cyrus nods his head slowly. "Okay. When can I read it?"

"When I'm finished."

"I guess you'll be Fawn when we film it."

"Of course."

"What's my part?"

Hmm. I hadn't thought of that. "Well, right now there are only two characters, and one of them is a dog named Arnold. I know! You can do Arnold's voice-over!"

"So, you can't even *see* me in this movie? Thanks a lot. And where are you going to get a dog, anyway?"

"I don't know yet, but I'm sure we'll figure it out. We must know somebody who has a dog. A big one. The bigger, the better."

A grin slowly spreads across Cyrus's face. "Gary Hackett," he says, "has a Saint Bernard."

★13★

"Maisie! Wait up!"

I know who it is without even turning around. I managed to avoid him at school yesterday, but I guess Tuesday is not my lucky day. Can I pretend I didn't hear him? I hook my arms through my backpack and wrangle my bike from the rack outside the school.

"Hold up, Maisie! I wanna talk to you!"

He knows I can hear him. How mean can I be?

"Oh, hey . . . " I almost say "Gary," but his name gets stuck in my mouth and I swallow it back down.

Hackett wheels his bike up next to mine. "Can I ride with you?"

What? "I'm not going home. I'm going to my grandma's."

"That's okay. I can ride anywhere I want as long as I don't cross Route 17."

I don't know what to say. I can't stop him, can I? So I just start riding, and he pedals right alongside me. I go faster, but he keeps up.

"Cyrus told me you're writing a movie," he says.

"A screenplay," I say. Does Cyrus have to tell this guy every single thing now?

"Right. A screenplay. He says it's kind of like *Harold and Maude*."

"Not really. I mean, that was just my inspiration."

"Cool." I speed up and he drops back for a minute, but before long he's next to me again. "Cy says you need a dog for the movie. Mine would be perfect."

We do need a dog. "Is yours big?" I ask.

"Huge. We named her Buffalo when she was a puppy, because, well, she kind of looks like a buffalo. But mostly we call her Buffy."

"Like *Buffy the Vampire Slayer*?"

"Yeah. Have you ever watched that show?"

"The early seasons," I say. "I liked it, but I stopped after Buffy died the second time."

"Yeah, it gets dark," said Hackett, "but it's still really good."

It's hard to pedal uphill and talk at the same time, but he's managing it without too much huffing and puffing. "Maybe you could come over to my house and see Buffalo sometime. You and Cyrus, I mean. She's a really smart dog."

"Maybe," I say.

He talks on and on about how enormous Buffy is, how much she eats, how his little sisters ride her around the house, and blah, blah, blah. I stop listening. How can a person be so cheerful and enthusiastic when they're being ignored?

"My little sister Abby is so funny. Once she put her hair barrettes all over Buffy, like twenty little bows and flowers and stuff, but Buffy didn't care . . ." It's nice that Hackett gets along with his little sisters, I guess, but how much information do I need to hear about them? This is the longest bike ride in history, but at last I see my grandma's condo at the end of the block. And there she is, sitting on the little porch, waving.

"Okay," I say to Hackett, dismissing him. "I guess I'll see you later."

Grandma stands up, leans over the porch railing, and squints at us. "That's not Cyrus, is it? Did you bring a new friend?"

"No, this isn't Cy. This is . . . um . . ."

"Gary Hackett!" he yells, as if she's deaf. "I met you once at Maisie's house."

"Well, I'm glad to see you again," Grandma says. "I love company. Come inside, both of you. I made brownies."

This cannot be happening. "But, Grandma, we have to work on my history project, remember?"

"There's plenty of time for that after we have our snack," she says.

In seconds Hackett manages to park his bike and chain it to the fence out front. He's up the steps and holding the door open for Grandma before I've even climbed off my bicycle.

By the time I get inside, Hackett is taking the tray of brownies to the table and yakking about how his mother never makes brownies even though they're his favorite food, and Grandma is telling him he should come over again and she'll make them for him whenever he wants. What the heck?

Grandma brings us big glasses of iced tea while I busy myself with the video camera. I watch as Hackett dumps six or seven spoonfuls of sugar into his tea.

"Sweet enough for you?" I ask.

He blushes, which makes me feel kind of bad for noticing his sugar consumption. And then bad for noticing the blushing, which actually makes him look kind of sweetly shy. It's possible I'm blushing now too. Apparently embarrassment is contagious.

"Did you say your name was Gary?" Grandma asks Hackett.

"Yup." His mouth is full of brownie.

"I've always liked that name. And anything that rhymes with it. Gary, Harry, Larry."

"My dad's name is Larry!" Hackett says, spitting chocolate crumbs all over the table in his excitement.

"Are you in Maisie's class at school?"

He nods. "We've been in the same class forever."

True, I think, but you didn't start bugging me until this year.

Grandma sighs. "You children are so fortunate to have your whole lives ahead of you. It's very exciting to be young! Soon you'll be falling in love and getting your heart broken and all those wonderful experiences."

Hackett chokes on his brownie and then has a coughing fit. Grandma whacks him on the back.

Oh my God, this has to stop. "Grandma," I say, "we need to get going on my history project. It's due next week, and I still have to edit it all together."

"Well, let's get to it then. I'm sure your friend won't mind listening to us talk, will you, Gary?"

"Not at all. My project is on my great-uncle Samuel. It's about how he was a pitcher in the minor leagues for the Decatur Commodores back in the sixties. You'd think that would be pretty interesting, but all he wants to talk about is how much beer they drank and how much tobacco they chewed. It's kind of gross."

Grandma laughs. "Well, I don't think my life is nearly as interesting as that. All I talk about is how I grew up working in my parents' grocery store."

"I'd like to hear about that," Hackett says politely.

I point the camera at Grandma and try to pretend he isn't sitting right here, listening and *liking* everything so much. "Why don't you tell me more about what you did with your girlfriends?" I ask her. "What did you do for fun besides go to the movies?"

She sighs and leans back in her chair. "We had good times. We played tennis and listened to records and danced. And we went to Turner's Swimming Pool as often as our parents would let us. You could get a pass for the whole summer."

"Were you a good swimmer?" I ask.

"Oh, no, not very. But we didn't go to swim. We'd just lie on our towels and slather ourselves with suntan oil—that wasn't so smart, but we didn't know it then." She dusts some brownie crumbs off the tablecloth into her hand, then gets up to throw them in the trash. I follow her with the camera. I'm glad she's moving around, because the film will be too static if she's sitting at the table the whole time. Also the light coming in the kitchen door throws a cool shadow when she stands near it.

Grandma laughs. "Some of the girls would parade around the pool in their swimsuits, trying to get the boys to notice them. And they did pay attention!"

For someone who was supposedly nervous around boys, she sure seems to want to talk about them a lot all of a sudden. "Did you have sleepovers with your girlfriends?" I ask, hoping to change the subject.

"Sometimes." She goes to the screen door, opens it a crack, and looks out. "My friend Laura came over a lot."

"Did you go out on dates?" Hackett asks, leaning his elbows on the table.

"Hey! This is my interview!" I look up from the camera to glare at him.

"Oh, sorry, Maisie," he says.

"We talked about that last time, when you weren't here," I tell him. "She didn't date anybody in high school. She was shy." Like I am, I think, but I don't say it.

Grandma is not paying attention to us anymore. She's mumbling something as she looks out the door.

"Is something wrong, Grandma?" I ask.

"I thought I heard him outside, but now I don't

see him," she says. "Soon as I shut the door, he'll be back here, scratching to get in."

"Your cat?" Hackett asks her.

Grandma nods. "He's an old rascal. We call him Batman because he's got a black mask on his face."

The pain in my chest is back, and I have to blink my eyes to keep the tears from leaking out while Hackett blabs on about his own cats. Apparently there's quite a menagerie over at his house, but not at my grandma's. Batman has been dead longer than Grandpa.

★14★

I should never have told Hackett, but he knew something was up when I wanted to leave Grandma's house so fast. Of course, he followed me home and kept asking questions, and finally—because I had to talk to somebody, and he was right there—I gave in and told him about Batman and the melted teakettle and Grandma mixing me up with my mother. And, of course, he was in the room the afternoon she forgot her husband was dead.

"Does your mom know?" he asks as we pull up in front of my house.

"I don't think so."

"You should tell her."

I'm thinking the same thing myself, but I don't like him telling me what to do. "I will," I say. "I just don't know if now's the right time. I mean, she's so busy, and my uncle's here with us, and—"

"If you wait, something could happen!" he says, his eyes getting big and damp. "My mom told me that my great-grandpa had Alzheimer's and he left home one night and got lost downtown. The police found him, but it was cold out and they said he could have frozen to death!"

"She's not going to freeze to death in May," I say. But the idea of Grandma getting lost and not knowing how to get back home suddenly stabs my heart like an icy knife. A tear rolls down my cheek. I turn away so Hackett doesn't see it, but apparently he never takes his eyes off me.

"I'm sorry, Maisie," he says. "I didn't mean to make you cry." His hand brushes against my shoulder, but he takes it back quickly. Maybe my skin has thorns. His touch is so light that I hardly feel it, and yet it reverberates through my whole body as if he's banged a gong deep inside me.

I brush the tear away and hope my voice isn't shaky. "I'm not crying. I'm just worried, is all."

"I know," he says. "I really like your grandma. She's got a wonderful laugh, and it was fun to hear her talk about growing up in New Aztec."

I nod, sniffling as quietly as I can.

"You're lucky you have such a great family, Maisie. I mean, your parents seem nice, and your uncle is super cool too."

"He really is," I say. Somehow Hackett has

made me feel okay again, like the ceiling hasn't just fallen in on my head.

Neither of us hears Cyrus walk up, and we jump a little when he says, "Hi."

I try to smile at him, but I can feel it's a cock-eyed smile.

"What's going on?" he asks, looking from one of us to the other. His face seems a little bit collapsed. Sad, I guess, or scared. He always knows what's going on with me, except right now he doesn't.

Hackett gives me a questioning look.

"Cy already knows most of it," I say. Then I tell him about the Batman episode. I can see he's relieved that Hackett and I aren't keeping some big secret from him.

"Wow," Cy says. "That's pretty crazy."

Crazy? "She's not crazy, Cyrus! There's something wrong with her."

"That's what I mean," he says. He looks up at Hackett and says, "She's gotta tell her mom now, don't you think?"

Hackett nods sadly.

"Okay. I know. I will." I take a deep breath and let it out in a big shuttering sigh. "I guess I might as well do it now."

Cyrus puts his hand on my shoulder, steady and strong, and gives me a little push toward my house. His hand landed on the same spot Hackett touched a minute ago, only there's no gong this time. It's confusing, but fortunately I have too much else on my mind to think about it for long.

"Good luck, Maisie," Hackett says.

"Thanks, Gary." I hardly even realize I've used his first name until I see Cyrus staring at me with a surprised look on his face. I guess he thinks it means something that I said "Gary" instead of "Hackett," but it doesn't. It's just that when someone is being nice to you, you can't very well keep calling him by his weird upchucked-hair-ball last name.

When I go inside, Uncle Walt is sitting at the dining-room table, flipping through a copy of *Entertainment Weekly* and looking glum. In the den, Mom's banging out (and belting out) "I Dreamed a Dream" from *Les Misérables*, a song sung by a woman whose life is hopelessly ruined. This can't be a good sign. I guess I should be glad she's not singing something from *Sweeney Todd*. Sometimes she really gets into those songs about the barber who slits people's throats and the cook who bakes them into pies.

I sit down across from Uncle Walt, who barely looks up.

"Has Mom been singing long?"

"One depressing dirge after the other for half an hour," he says.

"Any reason?"

He closes the magazine. "She got laid off. Something about budget cuts."

"Oh, no!" This isn't the first time it's happened. Mom used to be a receptionist for a law firm, but they had to lay off some people and decided they didn't need a receptionist anymore. She was out of work for eight months before she got the job as a parking enforcement officer, and those were long months. Dad was still working at the post office, of course, but we ate a lot of vegetable soup for dinner, and Mom walked around glaring at everybody like she was figuring out how many pies she could make out of them.

"She'll get something else," Uncle Walt says. "She always does."

But Uncle Walt wasn't here the last time this happened—he doesn't know how bad it gets. How can I tell Mom about Grandma now? But I have to, don't I? What if Gary's right and something terrible happens to her?

The den door slams, and I can hear Mom's bedroom slippers slogging toward us. She slides by without looking at us and goes into the kitchen.

When I get up to follow her, Uncle Walt says, "If I were you, I'd stay out of her way for a while."

"I don't think I can," I say. "I have something important to tell her."

"She's had enough important news for one day, Hitch."

I think that over. Should I wait until tomorrow? She'll still be laid off. I can't very well wait until she finds another job.

"It's about Grandma," I tell Uncle Walt.

He stares at me, his usual grin sagging at the corners and then collapsing altogether. A groan escapes him as he pushes back from the table and gets to his feet. "Okay. Let's do it."

Mom has ripped open a bag of potato chips and is sitting at the kitchen table, digging into it. Before I lose my nerve, I just start talking. "Something's wrong with Grandma," I say. "Today she thought her cat Batman was outside trying to get in." Mom stops chewing and stares at me. Her hand opens, and the chips she's holding fall back into the bag. Uncle Walt leans against the wall and puts a hand over his eyes.

I tell them about the other stuff—the teakettle and the mixed-up names. Mom's face gets pale, and she pushes the chip bag away from her like that's what's making her sick.

"I've seen a few things too," she says. "I guess I just didn't want to believe it. The other day I took her to the supermarket, and we got separated. I found her standing in the cereal aisle, crying because she couldn't find the Quaker Oats. This is the woman who didn't cry when her husband was diagnosed with lung cancer, and now she's in tears over a box of oatmeal. God, I didn't think this day could get any worse."

"I'm sorry, Mom. Uncle Walt told me you got laid off."

She puts her elbows on the table and lets her head fall into her hands. "Well, I guess the layoff came at the right time, huh? Now I can spend my days taking care of my mother as she gets more and more senile. She won't be able to live by herself. I'll have to move her in here with us. I'll be her caretaker for the rest of her life." She gives a terrible laugh. "Oh well, I've got no life of my own anyway."

Uncle Walt starts pacing around the table. "We'll figure something out, Cin. Maybe we can find a good nursing home someplace."

Mom's head jerks back. "*We'll* figure something out? Since when are you involved in taking care of your mother?"

"I always . . . You call me . . ."

And then Mom blows up. "Do you have any idea how much nursing-home care costs for somebody with dementia or Alzheimer's or whatever this is?"

Dementia. Alzheimer's. I never thought those words would refer to somebody in my own family. I wonder if that's what Jimmy Stewart had in

Harvey, the movie where his best friend was a giant, invisible rabbit. What's the difference between wacky and demented?

Mom is still ranting at Uncle Walt. "Carol Turner's father was in a nursing home for four years and it nearly bankrupted them, and they had more to begin with than we do. Mom's got nothing saved, and I just lost my job! Were you planning to contribute some of your tips from the Cheesecake Factory?"

I feel bad for Uncle Walt. When Mom gets crazy mad like this, she definitely seems like she wants to slit your throat. Uncle Walt glares back at her.

"That's not fair, Cindy. I've done what I could over the years. You're the one who lives here, so naturally the burden—"

"Not *fair*?" Mom jumps out of her chair, and for a minute I think she's going to attack her brother. He must think so too, because he turns to protect his bad side.

"You ran away to California to get rich and famous, to become Wade Wolf because even our *name* wasn't cool enough for you. And I was left behind to take care of our parents! I already nursed one of them through cancer, and now I have to deal with *this*! Don't tell me what's *fair*!"

"I came back when Dad was sick," Uncle Walt says, but I notice he's looking at the linoleum floor rather than into Mom's eyes. I remember Mom had to skip a lot of work when Grandpa was sick, which, now that I think about it, was right before she got laid off the first time.

"You came back for *one week*," Mom hisses at him. "Just in time to help me pick out the gravestone. Did you think this was how I wanted to spend my life, Walter? Stuck in this mud puddle of a town, dealing with all my mother's problems while she heaps praise on you, her beloved, runaway son? You knew I wanted a career in music. You just chose to forget about it."

Really? Mom wanted a music career? I never heard that before.

Now Uncle Walt is angry too, and he steps closer to her, sticking his finger in her face. "I did not run away. You're the one who dropped out of college to get married, Cindy! Don't blame me. I didn't tell you to stay in New Aztec and have a kid and lead such a boring life!"

And just like that, I'm in the fight too. Because I'm the kid who kept Mom stuck in New Aztec in "such a boring life." I feel like Uncle Walt has slapped me. He'd never do anything as foolish as having a kid like me and ruining his career. It's as if he threw a grenade and it hit me right in the chest.

Uncle Walt looks at me and holds out his hand. "I didn't mean—Maisie, you know I didn't mean . . ."

But I'm not listening anymore. I run out the back door so I can get far away from both of them before the explosion knocks me over.

I don't even think about where I'm headed, but I guess it makes sense that I end up in front of the Lincoln Theater, since it's my favorite place in town. Other people might go to a church when they're upset, but I believe in movies.

Tuesday matinees are usually musicals, and I see by the sign out front that today's is *The Sound of Music*. The show is just letting out, and a bunch of old people are getting into a van marked "St. Anthony's Elder Care" on the side.

It's mostly women, moving slowly, some of them with canes. In a race, Grandma would beat them easily. They don't look unhappy, but they also don't look like they're planning to climb every mountain until they find their dreams. They look like their dreams have been over for a long time.

Which ought to make me feel sad, I guess, but instead it makes me angry. I don't want my grandma's dreams to be over, or my mom's either, for that matter. Heck, I didn't even know my mom *had* dreams. How could I not have known that?

I pull the heavy door open and go into the lobby, where it's cool and smells like popcorn and bubble gum. Mr. Schmitz is running the vacuum cleaner over the lobby rug and doesn't hear me come in, so I sit on the stairs that go up to the balcony. He turns off the machine and wraps the cord around the handle, then looks over and sees me sitting there.

"Good Lord, when did you sneak in?" He puts his hand over his heart like I scared him, which I didn't mean to do. "The show's over already," he says. "You missed it."

"I know," I say. "Is it okay if I just sit here a minute?"

He gives me the side-eye. "Well, I'm closing the place up," he says. "But . . . you're the one, aren't you? You're Evie's grandkid."

I nod.

"How's she doing?"

I'm not sure how to answer that question. "Okay, I guess. But she's . . . starting to forget things."

Mr. Schmitz closes his eyes and screws up his

face like he's in pain. He turns away from me and says, "That's too bad."

"She still remembers stuff that happened a long time ago, though. She remembers you."

"I certainly remember her too," he says. He shakes his head and changes the subject. "You come here all the time, don't you? With that little boyfriend of yours."

"He's not my boyfriend. He's just my friend." Why do I have to keep explaining that to everybody?

"Yeah, okay." Mr. Schmitz scoots the vacuum cleaner across the rug and stashes it in a closet I never noticed before. "You two are real movie lovers."

"My uncle is an actor," I tell him. "He lives in Hollywood."

"What's his name?"

"Walter Hoffmeister. Well, his movie name is Wade Wolf."

He grunts. "Never heard of him."

"He hasn't gotten his big break yet."

Mr. Schmitz nods. "Say, you want some popcorn? It's not hot anymore, but I'm just gonna throw out what's left."

"Sure." I stand up and follow Mr. Schmitz to the counter. He goes behind it and gets a red-and-white box—one of the big ones—and loads it up to overflowing with popcorn, then drizzles butter all over it.

"You like butter, right?"

"Who doesn't?"

"Nobody I know," he says.

When I take the box from him, some of the top pieces fall onto the rug he's just vacuumed. He looks down at the escaped kernels but, surprisingly, doesn't mention it.

"So, you're a movie fan because your uncle's an actor, is that it?"

"Well, he got me started," I tell him. "But I think it was my destiny anyway. I'm going to be a director someday. Or at least a DP."

He looks surprised. "A DP?"

"Director of photography," I explain.

He gets this aggravated look on his face. If Mr. Schmitz was younger, he'd look like Bill Murray in *Groundhog Day*. "Yeah, I know what it is," he says. "I'm just surprised you know."

"I know a lot about film. I read books."

"Only so much you can learn from books," he says. "You wanna learn how to make a movie, make a movie. Get your hands dirty."

A few more kernels land on the rug, but Mr. Schmitz doesn't seem to notice. He's leaning on his elbows on the counter and looking into space.

"Oh, I intend to," I tell him. "I'm writing a script now. Did you ever make a movie?"

"I gave it a try," he says. "Not in Hollywood. Not

my style. But I was in New York for a while. When I was young."

"And you made movies?"

"Nothing big, but, yeah, I learned plenty."

"How come you didn't stay in New York? If I lived in New York and made movies, I wouldn't move back to New Aztec."

He straightens up and looks down at the counter, then grabs a rag and starts wiping the glass. "You're still a kid. You don't know what you'd do," he says. "Sometimes life turns you sideways. You make choices you didn't think you would."

I wonder if the way life turned him sideways had to do with Grandma or with that boy he tried to save from drowning, or if there were other sadnesses too.

He looks down and notices the popcorn scattered around my feet and turns back into crabby Bill Murray. "Did you not see me vacuum this rug ten minutes ago? Good Lord."

"I'll pick it up," I say, bending over. Unfortunately, when I bend over, I spill more out of the box.

Mr. Schmitz makes a shooing motion with his hands. "Just get out of the way! What are you hanging around here for, anyway? Take the popcorn outside, or I'll be sorry I gave it to you."

He heads for the hidden closet, and I go for the door. Oh, well. I've never talked to Mr. Schmitz for such a long time before. It was a pretty good conversation while it lasted. I'm pushing open the door when he calls after me.

"Say, does your grandmother have a telephone?"

"Yeah." Who doesn't have a telephone?

Mr. Schmitz clears his throat loud and long, as if he's about to say something important, but all he says is, "Do you happen to know the number?"

Everybody is in a terrible mood at dinnertime. We pick at our pasta and don't say much. Finally Dad stands up noisily from the table. He gives Uncle Walt a scornful look and says, "I'll get a second job, if I have to. You do what you have to do to take care of your family."

"Dennis, come on," Uncle Walt says. "I told you, I'm going to help out too."

"When have you ever helped us out, Walter? You come back here when you need something, not when we do. You'll go back to sunny California and forget all about what's happening back here." Dad stomps off into the kitchen. Mom flinches when his plate crashes into the sink.

"I mean it, Cindy," Uncle Walt says. "I'll help you. I don't know how yet, but I will. If I land this pilot and if the show sells, maybe I'll be able to—"

"If, if, maybe," Mom says, but she gives her brother a half-baked smile. "I know you mean well, Walt, and I'm sorry I got so mad at you this afternoon. You're right. I made my own decisions. I shouldn't whine about it now."

"Listen," Uncle Walt says, "I called Francine and told her she has to get me that Skype audition. She thinks she might be able to."

Mom shakes her head. "This can't wait until you land some great part. Mom can't be alone anymore. I need to find somebody to stay with her at her place when I can't be there. Then, when you go back to LA, I'll move her in here with us."

"In my room?" I ask quietly.

Mom nods. "I think so, Maisie. I'm sorry. It's got the air-conditioning, and it's close to the bathroom. You can fix up the den, though, so it feels like a bedroom. I'll move the piano out."

"Where?" I ask. Our house is small, and the rooms are pretty full already. I'm trying not to think about the wallpaper in my bedroom, which I chose myself when I was seven. It has green ferns that twist up the walls and make me feel like I'm sleeping in a garden. And I try not to think about the big window that looks out onto the backyard, where I watch the chipmunks stealing Mom's cherry tomatoes and sometimes baby rabbits coming out of their nest underneath the hosta plants.

The den has dark wood paneling, and you can only see the driveway from the one small window. But I know better than to complain about it, because everybody else is giving up things too. *It's for Grandma*, I tell myself. *You can give up your wallpaper for her.*

Mom sighs. "I should probably sell the piano. We could use the money, and I'm not going to have time to play it now anyway."

"No!" Uncle Walt yells, spraying iced tea across the table. "You can't sell your piano. I won't let you!"

Mom gives a sharp laugh. "You won't *let* me? You don't even like the music I play."

"Sometimes I do," he says. "Just not when you sound like Eeyore with his finger caught in a car door."

Mom's eyes open wide. "His *what* caught in a car door?"

"Okay, okay," Uncle Walt says. "Donkeys don't have fingers, but if they *did*!" Which makes us all, finally, laugh.

★★

Later on, Uncle Walt knocks on the den door and sticks his head in.

"Doing my homework," I say, although I finished

an hour ago. Mostly I'm sitting here thinking about the future and how much things are going to change, whether I want them to or not.

"Okay," Uncle Walt says. "I just wanted to tell you again how sorry I am about what I said this afternoon. You know that, right? I didn't mean your mom shouldn't have gotten married or had you or anything. You know I think you're the coolest kid since . . ." He stops to think. "Since Scout in *To Kill a Mockingbird*."

Uncle Walt is no dummy. He knows I love that movie, and especially Scout, who doesn't let anybody push her around. I almost smile, but I manage to stop myself. "Uh-huh," I say, not looking up.

He tries again. "You were always awesome, even as a little kid. You were willing to fight for what you wanted. I always said, 'Nobody puts Maisie in a corner!'"

I don't say anything, even though I catch the reference to *Dirty Dancing*, which Mom thinks I'm too young to see. Cyrus and I watched it at his house last year.

Uncle Walt sighs and comes farther into the room. "You're right. I don't deserve your immediate forgiveness. It's selfish of me to expect it." He gives a short laugh. "That's your mother's favorite word for me. Selfish. I guess I am."

I keep looking at the computer, and Uncle Walt wanders over to Mom's piano. He plinks around on it until he manages to play a stanza of "Mary Had a Little Lamb."

"I took lessons on this piano too," he says. "But I gave it up. It was too hard and I didn't like to sit still. Your mom, though, she was never happier than when she was sitting on this piano bench. She should have stayed in college or gone to a music conservatory or . . ."

Suddenly he bangs his fist on the piano keys, and the loud, jarring noise makes me jump. "This is why I don't like to argue with people," he says. "You say things you don't mean. Or, you kind of mean them, but the way you say it sounds arrogant and hurtful. And I never want to hurt your mom or you, Hitch. Especially not you."

That breaks me. I look up and smile. "I know."

He leans down to give me a sideways, injured-collarbone hug. "All I meant was we all make choices in life," he says. "I don't think your mom made bad choices. It's just . . . if you make a left turn, you can't make a right turn at the same time. You know what I mean?"

I nod, but I'm still confused. What if one person's choice ruins another person's chance to do what they dreamed of? If Uncle Walt hadn't left New Aztec for LA, would Mom have had a different life? If she hadn't stuck around here to take care of her parents, would she be a professional pianist now instead of an unemployed parking enforcement officer? If she hadn't married Dad, would I even have been born?

"Don't worry about it," I say. "I'm not mad at you anymore."

"Thanks, Hitch," Uncle Walt says. "Your mom has some old-fashioned ideas about obligation—how much people owe each other. I admire her, I really do, but I'm not that way. And maybe that's selfish or maybe it's just self-protective. Or maybe it's the same thing. Hey, I never said I was perfect."

He kisses the top of my head and leaves the room, but I can't stop thinking about what he just said. I guess I *did* think Uncle Walt was perfect, or as perfect as a person could be, and I don't like knowing he's not. And if I want to be just like Uncle Walt, does that mean I'm selfish too?

Cy is waiting for me after school on Friday. I can see his big grin from halfway down the hallway.

"Let's get going," he says. "Gary's bringing his dog over so we can see if he's right for the movie."

"The dog's a she," I correct him. "Buffy."

His grin disappears. "I thought it was Buffalo—that sounds like a boy. How do you know, anyway?"

"We talked about it the other day. It's Buffy for short."

He grunts. "I guess you guys talked about a lot of stuff the other day."

"Not really," I say. It's funny Cyrus is so bothered about me talking to Gary Hackett. I thought he *wanted* me to like the guy. Not that I like him all that much, of course.

Cy's mom is waiting for us in the car and starts

asking the usual mother questions: How was your day? How was the test? Do you have much homework? The kinds of questions that stop you talking about anything important.

When we get to Cy's, I run home and grab my camera, then join him on his front porch steps while we wait for Gary.

"So, what else did the two of you talk about?" Cyrus asks, pouting a little bit.

"Nothing! I told you already—my grandma and his dog." I'm looking at Cy's front yard through the camera, trying to see what might make an interesting background and where the best light is at this time of the day.

"I didn't even know you were hanging out now. I mean, I thought you didn't like him."

I put the camera down. "You're the one who told me to be nice to him! You said it was a compliment that he liked me, and I should stop being mean to him."

Cyrus stares between his shoes at the sidewalk. "I know. I just didn't think the two of you would suddenly be best buddies. Or whatever you are."

"We're not anything! We're just . . . people who talk to each other. Why are you being so weird? I thought you wanted me to like him."

"I did. I do. Just . . . "

"Just what?"

He shrugs. "I don't know."

And then I get it. Cyrus feels left out, like Gary is my new BFF or something. "Just because I talk to Gary once in a while doesn't mean anything is different between you and me," I tell him. "There's nobody I like more than you, Cy. I mean, you know, not *like* like."

He smiles a little and bumps his shoulder into mine. "Yeah, I know. You're right. Sorry I'm being weird."

"I'm used to it," I say, bumping him back.

Right about then a station wagon pulls up to the curb, and Gary Hackett gets out. Thank goodness he's wearing jeans today. There's a huge brown-and-white dog in the back of the car, slurping the window with a gigantic pink tongue.

Gary's mom gets out too. "Let me help you," she says. "Buffy gets really excited when she's been in the car, but she'll settle down in a minute."

Gary opens the hatch, and his mother grabs the leash just as Buffy leaps out of the car. The dog pulls her halfway across Cyrus's lawn before she gets enough leverage to yank her to a stop. I've never been afraid of dogs, but I wouldn't want to be run over by one this size.

"Sit, Buffy!" she yells. Buffy jumps up and puts her big paws on my shoulders, panting right in my face. Her doggy breath smells like the food you find in the back of the refrigerator that's been there so long you can't tell what it is anymore. I almost gag.

"Down, Buffy, down!" Mrs. Hackett says. "Just push her off you, dear."

It takes all my strength to get Buffy's feet back on the ground. Gary takes her leash and says, "Stay!" in a stern voice. Finally Buffy sits and stays, looking up expectantly. Gary pulls a treat from a bag he's wearing on his belt, and Buffy grabs it before he gets it anywhere near her mouth. She swallows it without even chewing.

"Now that she sees I've got the treats, she'll listen to me," Gary says.

"I hope so." His mother doesn't seem convinced. "My appointment should take about an hour. Then I'll come back for her," she says. "You'll be okay that long?"

"Of course," Gary says.

"Just don't let go of the leash," his mother warns him.

As she drives off, I start to realize how hard this is going to be. Arnold is a talking dog who has run away from home. He can't be wearing a leash in the movie, especially a leash with Gary Hackett attached to it.

"So when do we start making the movie?" Gary

turns in circles to keep Buffy away from the treat bag.

"I think we need to practice a few scenes with Buffy before we shoot anything," I say. "Do you think I could hold the leash?"

Gary looks uncertain. "I don't know. My mom said I should keep hold of it."

"I know, but in the movie the dog runs away with Fawn, with me. There can't be some guy along holding on to the leash."

"I'm not even in it," Cy says. "It's just a girl and a dog."

"Stop complaining," I tell him. "You're the dog's voice."

"Can I be in it?" Gary wants to know. "I could be a guy who also wants to run away. Then I could hold the leash."

Cy sticks his hands on his hips. "If Gary gets to be in it, so do I."

"I'd have to rewrite it completely!"

"You told me you didn't finish it yet. Come on! Let me and Cy be in it too," Gary begs. His eyes get all twinkly, as if he knows that will change my mind.

What can I do? If I'm going to have Buffy in the movie, it's pretty obvious I'll have to have Gary in it too. And I can't have Gary in it and not Cyrus, especially since he's been feeling left out lately.

"Maybe," I say. "Let me think about it."

"Yes!" Gary says. Apparently he's paying too much attention to me and not enough to Buffy. She grabs the treat bag right off his belt and chews up the whole thing in about two seconds. He tries to pull the bag out of her mouth, but all that's left are a few pieces of cloth.

"My mom's gonna kill me," Gary says, groaning. And then, while he's staring in horror at what's left of the bag, Buffy manages to jerk the leash out of his hands and starts galloping down the sidewalk.

"Buffalo!" he screams. "Catch her!"

Who would have thought that enormous fluffy cow could run so fast? She's headed right toward a little kid on a tricycle down the block, and he abandons his wheels and runs into his house, screaming. He probably thinks there's an actual buffalo on the loose.

The three of us chase after Buffy, but she's got a head start. Gary keeps yelling her name, which just seems to make her run faster. She gallops through Mr. Meyer's carefully tended peony garden, and pink petals float in the air like butterflies, then spin to the ground. Mr. Meyer is not going to be pleased.

Gary and I are neck and neck when all of a sudden Cyrus comes pounding around us with some kind of superhuman speed I didn't know he had. Just as he's catching up to her, Buffy veers off toward the street. Cy lunges at her and lands on top of her like a rodeo cowboy who's roped a calf. The two of them roll off the curb together.

"Grab the leash!" Cy yells, his fingers plunged deep into the giant fur ball's coat. He's got peony petals in his hair, and Buffy's got one on her nose.

Gary gets the leash and wraps it around his hand twice. "Got it! Wow, thanks, Cy. She could have gotten hit by a car!"

"When did you become a sprinter?" I ask Cyrus as I help him up.

Cy dusts off his pants and shrugs. He seems a little embarrassed by his accomplishment. "I don't know. It was an emergency, so I ran fast."

Buffy trots happily down the sidewalk. Apparently she's already forgotten about her race for freedom. When we get back to Cy's front yard, she scarfs down the last few treats that fell onto the grass.

Cyrus plops down next to Buffy, and she slurps his face with her gigantic tongue. "Pew! What do you feed this dog? Garbage and skunks? Maisie, why did you have to write a story about a dog, anyway?"

"You're just mad she has a bigger part than you do," I say.

"Yeah, I am! If I'm gonna spend the summer making this movie, I at least want to be in it."

"Come on, Maisie," Gary says. "Let's rewrite it so there are parts for all of us. We'll do it together."

I give up and sit down next to Cy. I can't make a movie by myself. I can't make a movie with a dog in it if I don't have a dog. Sometimes you can't make the exact movie you have in your mind, so you make the movie you *can* make. I'm sure some famous filmmaker said that sometime.

Buffy throws up and then falls fast asleep on the lawn.

Cy brings his mother's laptop outside and types away as we come up with ideas. We decide to go back to the ghost idea, so okay, there will be three ghost kids and one ghost dog. That could be funny, right? And maybe a little scary too.

"So, are we brothers and sisters or what?" Gary asks. "I mean, we don't look much alike."

"How about cousins," I say. "Cousins don't have to look alike. And Uncle Walt can be our uncle."

Cyrus nods. "Yeah, he's too good-looking to be believable as the father of one of us."

Gary gives Cy an elbow in the ribs, but he laughs too. "Speak for yourself, dork."

Cy's face turns red.

"He could be Maisie's father," Gary says, looking across Cy and down toward me. "You both have dark hair and . . . stuff."

"We're getting off track," I say, to change the subject from my "stuff." "We have to decide who can see the ghosts. Just Uncle Walt, or whatever we're going to call him? Or can other people see us too?"

"It would be funnier if other people could see us too," Cyrus says. "We could scare them."

"But not everybody," Gary says. "Just some people."

"So, why can some people see us and others can't?" I ask.

We think about that for a minute, and then it comes to me. "The people who were kind to us when we were alive can see us, but mean people can't. That way we can pull tricks on them, and they won't know who did it."

"Yeah, but if the nice people can see us, they're the ones getting scared," Cy says.

"Just at the beginning," I say, "but then they figure out we're not going to hurt them. It'll be funny."

"Yeah, Maisie's right," Gary says, smiling at me.

The three of us manage to figure out a plot pretty quickly. I don't mind so much that Gary Hackett is part of our group now, which might be because of how he agrees with pretty much everything I say. If Cy and I are arguing about something, Gary is always on my side. "We could make up our faces to look all bloody and weird," Cy says, excited. There's nothing he likes more than face paint, which you can tell from every Halloween picture his mother has ever taken.

"Cyrus, we're supposed to be ghosts, not zombies!" I say. Gary cracks up laughing like I'm Tina Fey or Melissa McCarthy. It's a little embarrassing, but it's also pretty cool that he thinks I'm funny.

It's strange having somebody like me so much. It makes me feel a little bit . . . powerful. Like I'm making it happen. I'm sitting here with two boys, and suddenly I feel almost like a different person. I mean, I feel like such a *girl*. I never felt like this when it was just me and Cy.

Cyrus doesn't laugh—he just looks at the computer. "Okay," he says, "we need to scare somebody. Oh, you know what would be funny? Maybe Buffy scares some other dogs!"

I do think that would be funny, but I've already got another idea, so I say, "How about this? Let's scare Mr. Kane! We won't even tell him he's in a movie!" Mr. Kane is the vice-principal at our school. He's always staring at kids in the hall and poking two fingers at his own eyes and then at yours. He's creepy.

"That's awesome, Maisie!" Gary yells. "It would be so hilarious to scare Mr. Kane!"

Cyrus smacks the laptop shut and jumps up.

"You think everything Maisie says is so great, Gary! You don't even listen to what I say! My ideas are just as good as hers!"

Whoa. Cyrus doesn't get mad very often, which makes it so much worse when he does. He looks like he's trying really hard not to cry, and I don't know what to say. Why is he getting so upset about everything these days?

Gary is surprised too. "I didn't mean your ideas weren't good, Cy."

"I liked your dog idea," I say. "I just thought of that Mr. Kane thing—"

But Cy isn't looking at or listening to me. His eyes are locked on Gary's, and his face is on fire. "I guess you two would rather do this without me," he says. "I'm just getting in your way. I'm just the dogcatcher."

"I didn't say that—" Gary says. "You guys are the moviemakers. I just—"

But Cyrus is heading for his front door, fast.

"Cy, come on!" I yell. "What's the matter? We want to do this with you!"

I'm pretty sure there are tears spurting from his eyes by now, and there's no chance he'll turn around and let us see that. He slams the door behind him.

Gary stares at me in shock. "What just happened? Why is he so mad?"

I shrug like I don't know either, but I do know, and I feel bad about it. I liked the way Gary thought everything I said was hilarious, and I wasn't really paying much attention to Cyrus's ideas. It was almost like Gary and I were in a little circle that Cy was locked out of. I never meant to hurt Cyrus's feelings. Maybe he thinks I don't want to be his best friend anymore. I'll explain it to him. We'll make up. We always do.

Gary is pulling up chunks of grass from the lawn. "If Cyrus doesn't want to make the movie anymore, I guess we'll have to do it ourselves. I mean, the two of us, together." He looks up at me shyly.

What? No, no, no. I mean, Gary's okay. I even kind of like him now, but there is no "two of us, together." No way.

"I'll talk to Cyrus," I say. "I'll make him change his mind."

"Well, if he doesn't *want* to—"

"He wants to," I say. "Cyrus and I always want to make movies together. Maybe the *three* of us wasn't such a good idea."

Gary's tentative smile crumbles, which makes me feel kind of lousy. I like Gary now, but I need Cyrus to be part of this too. Cy is my best friend, always and forever. And Gary doesn't want to be my best friend—he wants something else, something I don't even want to think about. We sit in silence for a few more minutes, ripping bald patches in Cy's parents' lawn until Mrs. Hackett pulls up in the station wagon and the big pillow we've been leaning on leaps up, barking, and runs to greet her.

"Everything good with Buffy?" Mrs. Hackett asks.

Gary nods.

"She was perfect," I say.

Mrs. Hackett laughs. "That's a first."

Gary gets up and heads to the car. "See you, Maisie," he says sadly.

"Okay," I yell after him. "See you!" I try to sound enthusiastic, but he doesn't turn around.

While his mom loads Buffy into the back, Gary gets into the front seat and slams the door.

I turn around and look at Cyrus's front door, also slammed. An hour ago we were having a great time, and now everybody's mad at everybody. I hate being twelve.

★19★

"Hurry up, Maisie," Mom calls. "I want to have time to explain everything to Grandma before the caretaker gets there."

Mom is already outside, waiting by the car, when I shuffle out. "Why do I have to go with you? Why can't Uncle Walt?" The Saturday matinee is *Dracula*, the 1931 version with Bela Lugosi, and I know Cyrus wants to go. It might have been an easy way to patch up the weird argument we had yesterday, but I didn't call him since I had to go to Grandma's today, and he didn't call me either.

Mom doesn't answer my question right away. We're a block or two down the street before she says, "I don't really want your uncle Walt along. And anyway, he didn't want to come."

I can understand why he didn't want to come; explaining to my grandmother that her memory is so bad that she has to have a total stranger stay with her isn't high on my list of favorite ways to spend the afternoon either.

"Why don't you want Uncle Walt along? Grandma's crazy about him."

"Exactly. And it turns us both into our worst selves. When Grandma starts in on how fabulous Walter is, he becomes a preening prima donna and I turn into a resentful, fire-spewing dragon."

"I guess you get jealous."

"I do, Maisie, and I'm not proud of it. Anyway, today isn't about me or your uncle Walt. It's about getting your grandmother to accept something she's not going to like. I want to concentrate on that problem and not my own."

I can see why Mom gets jealous. Grandma does act like Uncle Walt is her favorite child, but I always figured that was just because he's not around much. She misses him, plus he's not here to argue with her like Mom is.

"So how come I have to go?" I ask.

"Because Grandma adores you too, and I'm hoping that will make this easier. It won't be just me, the bad guy, delivering the news. You'll help soften the blow."

"But you're not jealous of me?"

She laughs. "Of course not, Maisie. You're my daughter!"

I don't know why that makes a difference, but I let it go.

"It's just that I really wanted to go to the movies today."

Mom sighs. "Maisie, you go to the movies every Saturday. It won't kill you to miss a week."

"I didn't say it would *kill* me," I mumble.

Mom is quiet a minute, and then she says, "What is it you love so much about movies, anyway?"

Wow, she's never asked me that before. "I'm not sure I can explain it to you," I say.

"Just try," Mom says. "I'm interested."

It's cool that Mom wants to know, so I try to say clearly what I think. "In a theater, when you're sitting in the dark, you forget where you are. It's like I'm not in New Aztec anymore. I'm in London or Wyoming or New York City or even the Civil War or outer space, and I'm imagining what it would be like to be one of the characters who live there."

Mom nods. "You're taken out of yourself. I understand that. Music does a similar thing for me."

I'm kind of thrilled that she gets it, so I keep talking. "And I like the way movies look, the way all the action takes place inside a frame. You only see what the director wants you to see, the world inside the frame. It's like you're inside the director's head."

"I never thought of it that way," Mom says.

"And I love that there have to be so many people involved to tell one story," I say. "Everybody has to believe in the same thing: writers and casting agents, makeup and costume people. The cinematographer and the grips and gaffers—those are the lighting people—and the prop people, set decorators, sound technicians, and camera operators, and the actors of course. And then the director and the assistant directors oversee the whole thing. And even after that there are editors in postproduction who put it all together and make it a movie."

Mom laughs. "It makes me wonder how movies ever get made. But you don't really think about all those things when you're watching a movie, do you?"

"Not all of them all the time, but some of them some of the time. The more you know, the more you enjoy the film."

Mom nods. "It's not so different from music in that way either." She glances over at me. "Thanks for telling me why you're so passionate, Maisie. I'm sorry now I made you miss your movie this afternoon."

"You know," I say, "you should ask Uncle Walt sometime why he's so passionate about acting."

Mom smiles, but she doesn't look at me and she doesn't answer.

We're quiet a few minutes, and then I say, "I never knew you wanted to be a musician. Why did you give it up?"

"I didn't give it up," she says. "I still play."

"Yeah, but . . ."

"Maisie, we don't all get to do exactly what we want. I don't have to be a famous pianist to be happy. I married your dad and I had you. That's a good enough life for me."

Good enough? "Couldn't you have had both?"

She's quiet for a long time, and then she says, "I didn't think so at the time."

★★

When we get to Grandma's place, there's a car parked outside we don't recognize. "Oh, no," Mom says. "The caretaker must have gotten here early. I told her two o'clock."

"Does Grandma really need to have somebody living with her all the time?" I ask. "Somebody she doesn't even know?"

Mom nods. "It's too dangerous for her to be alone anymore. And who knows? Maybe this woman and Grandma will really hit it off."

We knock on the door, then push it open and go in. There are voices coming from the kitchen, so Mom hurries in that direction, with me behind her. But the person sitting at the kitchen table with Grandma is not the new caretaker.

"Oh, Cindy, I didn't know you were coming!" Grandma says. "I'll make more tea."

She gets up and heads for the stove as Mr. Schmitz rises from his chair and puts out a hand toward Mom. "Hello," he says. "I'm Hank Schmitz. You must be Evie's daughter." His gruff voice is a little softer than usual.

Mom doesn't know what to say, but she shakes his hand.

"Hi, Mr. Schmitz," I say. He raises a hand in my direction. If you didn't know better, you'd think he was a pretty friendly guy.

Mom looks at me. "How do you know—?"

"Mr. Schmitz owns the Lincoln Theater," I tell her.

"Oh, of course," Mom says. "I recognize you now."

"Your daughter's my best customer," he says. Then he looks at me. "Why aren't you there today? It's *Dracula*, you know."

"Why aren't *you* there?" I say. "You're always there on Saturday."

"Maisie, don't be rude!" Mom puts a hand on my shoulder.

Mr. Schmitz grunts. "Well, if you must know, Sherlock, I hired somebody to help out so I could get away once in a while." There he is. That's the Mr. Schmitz I know.

"Hank and I are old friends," Grandma says. "I was so happy when he called and asked if he could come over." She's trying to pour hot water from a big pot into two little cups, which reminds Mom why we came in the first place. She runs over and takes the pot from Grandma's hands.

"Let me do that."

"What kind of tea do you—"

"I'll get the tea, Ma. You just sit down now."

"Oh, for heaven's sake." Grandma shakes her head and returns to the table. "You're certainly bossy today, Cindy. Did I know you were coming? I don't remember."

"I told you yesterday," Mom says. She brings the cups to the table.

"It must have slipped my mind. It's funny. Sometimes I can hardly remember what happened an hour ago, but when Hank and I start reminiscing about things that happened fifty years ago, I remember it all perfectly!" She reaches across the table and puts her hand on his, and I think Mom's eyes are going to fall out of her head and roll around on the table.

"Well, it's nice you've reconnected with your old friend," Mom says, "but I need to talk to you about something today, Ma. It's kind of important."

"I can't imagine what's so important we have to interrupt my conversation with Hank." Grandma's eyes flash at Mom, but then I think she looks a little scared.

Mr. Schmitz immediately stands up. "Well, I should get going anyway."

"No! Don't leave!" Grandma shouts, and then she stands up too. "I don't want you to go yet, Hank."

"I'll come back and visit you again, if you want, Evie. Your daughter wants to talk—"

Grandma's eyes fill with tears, and she grabs Mr. Schmitz's hand in both of hers and brings it to her cheek. "I don't care what she wants. I want you to stay!"

Whoa! I can hardly remember Grandma ever touching Grandpa, except maybe to smack him on the shoulder to get his attention if his hearing aids were turned off. But now she's gripping Mr. Schmitz's hand and looking up at his face like she's Cher and he's Nicolas Cage in *Moonstruck*. Like she's Julie Christie and he's Omar Sharif in *Doctor Zhivago*. Like she's Lady and he's the Tramp. And Mr. Schmitz doesn't seem to mind at all, which makes me like him a little more than I did before.

Mr. Schmitz looks at Mom. He seems embarrassed but also calm. "Maybe it would help if I stayed. We've been having such a nice visit."

Mom looks like she's been kicked in the head by a mule. "Well, I don't know . . . I suppose if she . . . if you . . ." She gives up on that sentence.

When Mr. Schmitz sits back down, Grandma does too. She sips her tea as if nothing strange has happened. "So now, what's so darned *important*, Cindy?"

Mom takes a deep breath and begins. "The thing is, you've been having some memory problems lately, Ma, and Walt and I have been talking—"

"Oh, wait until you meet my son, Walter," Grandma says to Mr. Schmitz. "You'll like him. He's full of fun!"

"I believe your granddaughter told me about him," Mr. Schmitz says. "An actor, isn't he?"

"That's right! He and Maisie are two peas in a pod."

Mom looks at me like *Why are you having conversations with old men in movie theaters?* But then she remembers her point. "Anyway, Ma, you're forgetting things, and Walt and I think there should be someone around here to help you. Sort of a companion."

Grandma gives a sharp laugh and shakes her head. "That's the silliest thing I ever heard. I don't need any help. And I certainly don't want somebody I don't know following me around my own house!"

"She won't follow you, Ma. She'll just be here if you need her."

"Well, I *don't* need her. I don't need anybody! If I needed someone, I'd call you. Or . . . maybe I'll call Hank. Can I call you if I need help, Hank?"

Mr. Schmitz reaches across the table and takes Grandma's hand. "Of course you can, Evie. Whenever you need me, I'll come right over."

Mom looks like she walked in on the middle of a movie and can't figure out what's going on. Finally she says, "Look, Hank, I'm sure you mean well, but my mother is having severe memory issues, and I need to do something about it. She thinks she can call people for help, but she won't remember our numbers. I don't know if she can even remember how to use the telephone!" Suddenly Mom puts her hands over her face and starts to cry.

"Oh, for goodness' sake, Cindy," Grandma says, "get ahold of yourself. Of course I can use a telephone. What's wrong with you today?"

There's a knock on the front door and Grandma gets up to answer it, but Mom leaps to her feet too, wiping the back of her hand over her face. "No, wait! That's her. That's Mary Jane."

"Mary Jane who? I don't know any Mary Jane," Grandma says.

"She's your new . . . companion."

Grandma stares at Mom. I'm glad she's never

stared at me like that; her angry look burns like fire.

"Well, tell her to go away," Grandma says.

"I can't," Mom says. "I've already hired her and—"

"Anybody home?" A heavy, middle-aged woman in purple yoga pants and a matching sweatshirt prances into the kitchen. She looks a little bit like Robin Williams in *Mrs. Doubtfire*. "I thought maybe you couldn't hear me. You all were making so much noise in here." She sticks out a big paw toward Grandma. "I'm Mary Jane. You must be Evelyn."

Grandma's arms remain at her sides, and the look in her eyes could boil water. Mary Jane takes back her unshaken hand and looks around the kitchen as if she owns the place already and is imagining herself cooking at the stove and washing up dishes at the sink.

After a few seconds I hear a sound that seems to be coming from Grandma's belly. It rises up through her throat and comes spilling out of her mouth in the loudest shriek I've ever heard. "Get out of my house!" she yells. When Mary Jane doesn't move but continues to stand there with a silly grin on her face, Grandma throws herself against the woman's chest as if she's going to *push* her out.

Mary Jane keeps her feet planted like a tree and doesn't move. "Oh, dear, we need to calm down," she says. Then she puts her hand up to cover part of her mouth and whispers loudly to Mom, "Don't worry. I've had ornery ones before."

"She isn't ornery—she's just upset," Mom says as she tries to put herself between the two of them.

Mr. Schmitz stands up, takes Grandma by the shoulders, and pulls her back. Mary Jane brushes at her sweatshirt as if Grandma has gotten it dirty. "Probably time to get her on some meds," she says.

Mom takes Mary Jane by the elbow and leads her into the living room. "Let's talk in private for a minute."

Grandma curls into Mr. Schmitz's chest, and he puts his arms around her. "I don't want that woman in my house!" she says. "I don't want anybody in my house! Just you, Hank. Just you. Tell the rest of them to go away."

"Shh. It's okay, Evie," he says. "Don't worry. I'll take care of you."

The crabby old guy from the Lincoln Theater has disappeared. Mr. Schmitz's voice is soft, and his lower lip is trembling. He reminds me of Robin Williams at the end of *Dead Poets Society*—there's a little smile on his face, but you know he's actually as sad as he's ever been in his whole life.

"I'm glad I was able to explain things to Mary Jane. I think she'll be able to handle the situation, don't you?" Mom has been talking nonstop the whole car ride home, usually to herself, but once in a while to me too.

"Maybe," I say. Actually I don't have high hopes for Mary Jane. She seems like someone who wants to be the boss, which is a job Grandma isn't going to hand over to anybody else. Grandma let us make Mary Jane a cup of tea, finally, but she didn't want her to sit at the table with us. She made her sit across the room in a chair Mr. Schmitz brought in from the porch.

"I don't understand why this Hank person is suddenly on the scene," Mom says. "How did he even find her?"

"I guess I gave him her phone number," I admit.

The car swerves as we turn onto our street. "You gave him her phone number! Why?"

"I told you. Grandma said they liked each other when she was young. Before she met Grandpa. She danced with Mr. Schmitz once and she even kissed him."

Mom stares at me with her mouth hanging open. I hope she doesn't hit a parked car. "That was a million years ago. I didn't think she still knew him! She *kissed* him?"

"Just once. She didn't see him for a long time because Grandpa didn't like him. I guess he was jealous."

"I still don't understand why you gave him her phone number."

"When I told Grandma I knew Mr. Schmitz from the Lincoln, she said to say hello to him from her. Which I did. And then, I don't know, he stopped being so crabby. He got kind of almost . . . nice. Well, not all the time, but once in a while. So when he asked me for her number . . . should I not have given it to him?"

Mom pulls into our driveway and turns the car off. "Oh, I don't know, Maisie. He seemed kind this afternoon, but I'm so confused by all of this. It's very odd to see my mother acting like a lovesick teenager with some man I hardly know."

I'm still listening to Mom, but my eyes are on

Cyrus and Gary, sitting on the porch at Cy's house. "I think she's probably the same person she always was," I say. "Only now she's more like the young person than the old person. At least in her mind."

Mom squeezes my shoulder, but she doesn't say anything. Her eyes look puffy.

"Can I go over to Cy's?" I ask.

She nods. "Thanks for coming with me today, Maisie. Having you there was a big help."

"No problem, Mom." I open the door and scoot out before she starts crying or hugging me or something.

I'm glad to see that Gary and Cyrus are laughing. They're leaning against the porch posts and bouncing a tennis ball back and forth between them. But the minute Cy sees me coming, his smile disappears and he lets the tennis ball drop into the bushes. *What?* He's not mad at Gary, but he's still mad at me?

Gary looks pretty happy to see me, though. "Hey, Maisie! We missed you. *Dracula* was awesome—you should've come!"

"I wanted to, but I had to go to my grandma's."

"Hey, what happened with her? Did you tell your mom about the cat thing?" His eyebrows bunch up and he looks worried, as if he actually cares about my grandma. Yeah, I have to admit Gary Hackett is okay.

"That's where we were this afternoon. Grandma's new caretaker came over for the first time, and Grandma did *not* like her. She screamed at her, and pushed her, and then she started crying." Why am I telling him the whole story?

"Oh, wow. That sounds bad." He reaches out a hand and lays it carefully on my arm. I can tell he's ready to remove it immediately if I jerk away or anything, so I stand still as a statue. The heat from his fingers brands my skin.

For a minute I even forget Cyrus is sitting there until he says, "Your mom's here, Gary," in this voice that sounds like he's just swallowed a handful of nails.

Mrs. Hackett's station wagon idles in the driveway.

"Shoot. Why does she always have to be on time?" Gary says. His fingers loosen on my arm and take their warmth with them. "Maybe I'll see you guys tomorrow," he says, but he's only looking at me.

"Maybe," I say. Cy doesn't say anything. He doesn't even look at Gary. And the minute Gary disappears into his mother's car, Cy gets up and heads for the front door.

"Wait a minute, Cyrus. What's going on? How come you're still mad at me but not Gary?"

"I don't want to talk about it," he says, but at least he doesn't run inside.

"Well, you have to talk about it! We're making a movie together. I don't want to do it with only Gary."

"Maybe not, but Gary wants to do it with only you." He plops down on the top porch step and watches Gary's mother's car disappear down the street.

"No, he doesn't," I say, though I have a feeling Cy might be right. "And anyway, I don't care what Gary wants. We're best friends, Cy. We always will be."

"Maybe, maybe not," he says. He balances his arms across his knees and lets his head drop onto them.

I'm so stunned, I don't say anything for a minute. I sit down next to him, and I want to put my arm around him because obviously something is really, really wrong, but I'm kind of afraid to touch him. There's something so fragile about him right now that a touch might break him completely.

"You don't want to be my best friend anymore?" My voice trembles in a way I can't hide.

"I can't talk about this with you, Maisie. You wouldn't understand."

"Cyrus, I know you better than anybody. You can tell me anything!"

"Not this."

Now I'm getting kind of mad. Why doesn't he trust me? "Cyrus, you're the one who said keeping a secret is like lying, especially if it's about something important. If you can't tell me, you can't tell anybody!"

Finally he picks his head up and looks at me. He's not crying, like I thought he might be. He sticks out his chin like Willem Dafoe in *The Grand Budapest Hotel*, trying to look furious and mean. Though actually he looks more like James Dean in *East of Eden*, who's trying to look tough but is obviously all torn up inside. "That's right," he says. "I can't tell anybody."

Of course I'm not giving up that easily. "Does it have something to do with Gary? You never acted this way until he started hanging around with us. If you want me to tell him we don't want to hang out with him anymore, I will."

Then his face kind of crumbles, and he gives me the most miserable smile I have ever seen. "Oh, Maze, I'm sorry."

"What are you sorry for? Cyrus, come on. Tell me!"

He looks into my eyes for a few long, terrible seconds, and then he says, "You can't tell anybody. Ever."

"Of course I won't tell anybody. You know I won't!"

"It's not just some silly secret. I really mean it, Maisie. Nobody else knows about this. You can't tell *anybody*."

"I get it, Cy. Just tell me."

He looks away and takes a deep breath. When he finally speaks, it's so quiet I can't hear him.

"What?"

"I said, I like Gary."

"I know you like Gary. You liked him before I did."

He stares at me. "I *like* like him."

For a minute I don't know what he means. It doesn't make any sense to me, and then all of a sudden it does.

"You mean you're . . . *gay*?"

He turns around and looks at the door of his house. "Not so loud. My mom is home."

I don't know what to say. I thought I knew everything about Cyrus, but all of a sudden it seems like I don't know him at all.

"I don't know if I'm gay," he whispers. "Maybe I am. I just know I really like Gary and he really likes you. I thought at first that would be okay, that we'd kind of all like each other, but it's not okay. I can't stand it, Maisie. When I see how he looks at you, it makes me feel awful. I want him to look at me like that, and I know he never will."

I didn't think Cyrus could ever tell me anything I didn't want to know. But all of a sudden, he's definitely giving me too much information.

I stand up. "I should go home," I say. When I glance at Cy, he's glaring at me.

"You're going *home*?" His mouth drops open. "Maisie, I just told you a huge secret. You're just going to walk away? I knew I shouldn't have told you."

"Well, maybe you should have told me sooner. Before I . . ."

"Before you *what*?"

"Never mind."

"Before you started liking Gary too?" I can hear the tears in his voice, and I wonder if he can hear them in mine.

"No. Just . . . I don't know what to say, Cy. You surprised me. I have to think about it."

We stare at each other as if we can see underneath the other person's skin. Finally Cyrus says, "You're not going to tell anybody, are you?" He sounds so scared, I have to turn away.

"Of course not. I said I wouldn't, and I won't." I glance back at him. "Cy, are you *sure*?"

He shakes his head. "I'm not sure about anything, Maisie. I'm so confused, my stomach hurts all the time. When I'm alone with Gary, I feel like I might throw up."

I remember the way I felt when Gary touched my arm. Yup, there was definitely some stomach upset involved there too. How can this be true? How can Cyrus like the same boy who—okay, I admit it—I like too? I *like* like. And if Cy is gay, why didn't I know it before now?

★146★

"I'll talk to you tomorrow," I say. "I just have to think about all this."

Crouched on the steps, Cy looks up at me as if he's Elliott and I'm E.T. and I just told him I'm returning to my own planet forever. "I know you're freaked out," he says. "I get it. I'm freaked out too."

"I'm not freaked out. I just . . . I just have to go!" I do. I have to. I can't think it through with him sitting right there.

As I run across the street to my house, I can feel Cyrus's sorrow attaching itself to me. I'm not going to be able to outrun it.

I stay up for all of *Saturday Night Live*, but even Kate McKinnon and Kenan Thompson can't get my mind off all the changes going on. Mom losing her job, Grandma losing her memory, and now this: my best friend telling me a secret that's going to change everything for him. And maybe for me too. Can we still be best friends, or am I going to lose Cyrus now too?

I think about some of the movies Cy checked out of the library the last few months. We both thought *The Birdcage* was hilarious, and we laughed at *The Adventures of Priscilla, Queen of the Desert* too, until one of the guys got beaten up. And I cried more than Cy did over *Philadelphia* when the Tom Hanks character was dying of AIDS. But I never thought it meant anything that Cy picked those movies. Maybe it didn't. They all had interesting screenplays and terrific actors. So, were there any signs? If there were, I must have missed them.

I'm finishing up my scrambled eggs Sunday morning when Gary calls. I've never talked to a boy on the phone before except for Cyrus, and it makes me nervous. It's worse than talking to somebody in person because you can't see what their face looks like. You can't tell if they're nervous too, and you can't try to figure out what they're going to say next.

"Hey, Maisie," Gary says. "I was wondering what you were doing today. I thought maybe I could come over or something."

"Come over? To my house, you mean?" What else would he mean?

"Yeah, just for a little while. Maybe this afternoon. We could take a walk or something."

"Oh." My stomach gurgles, and I wish I hadn't slugged down that orange juice. "Well, the thing is, I have to edit my history project today. You know, the movie I made about my grandma. It's due tomorrow."

"Oh, right."

There's a long silence. No way am I going to hang out with Gary after what Cyrus told me yesterday. Uncle Walt is watching me from the table, which makes me even more fidgety.

Finally Gary says, "Maybe I could help you with your project." He doesn't sound too hopeful.

"I don't think so," I say. "I have to write up a report about it too. It's probably going to take me all day." Can he tell I'm lying? I can probably get the whole thing done in a few hours.

There's a big sigh on Gary's end. "Okay. I guess I'll just see you at school tomorrow, then."

I know he's disappointed, but what can I do? Now that I know about Cyrus's feelings, I'm even more confused about Gary. Cy's hurt when the guy talks to me—how bad would he feel if Gary was my boyfriend? I'm not sure I want that anyway.

"Yup, I'll see you at school!" I say in my breeziest voice. "Bye!" I click off the phone and go back to the table. I hope Uncle Walt can't tell my heart is beating way too fast.

"What was that about?" he says.

It's just the two of us having breakfast. Mom already left for Grandma's house to check on Mary Jane, and Dad went to Baldwinville to look at a truck he'd like to buy.

"Nothing," I lie.

"Didn't sound like nothing."

"It was just Cy, as usual." I always tell Uncle Walt the truth, and now suddenly I'm a serial liar.

Uncle Walt has a know-it-all smile on his face. "That was not Cyrus."

"How do you know?"

"Because you don't get all fluttery when Cy calls."

"What? I didn't 'get all fluttery.'" I can feel my face heating up. It's not as good a liar as the rest of me.

"Okay, Hitchcock," he says, leaning back in his chair. "Keep your secrets."

If only I didn't have to. Not just this little secret, but the other enormous one. I wish I could talk about it with somebody who knows more about this stuff than I do, but I can't. I promised.

The rest of my eggs are cold and rubbery now. There's no way I'm putting those into my jumpy stomach.

"I guess Cy's coming over to help you with your project," Uncle Walt says. "The two of you never go a whole weekend without hanging out."

I get busy spreading cream cheese on my bagel, as if it's necessary to cover every toasty crumb. "He's busy today," I say. "I think his dad's taking him fishing or something." Oh my God, I'm incorrigible.

"I don't think so," Uncle Walt says. "I saw his dad drive off about an hour ago, and Cy's been sitting out on his front porch alone."

"What are you, the neighborhood spy?" It comes out sounding nastier than I expect it to.

Uncle Walt narrows his eyes and leans across

the table. "Okay, Maisie, what's going on? Are you still mad at me? I get it if you are, but—"

"That's not it," I tell him, although maybe a little part of me *is* still mad. Once somebody says something that hurts you, you can't forget about it right away, even if you want to. Which is one reason I don't want to talk to Cyrus until I know what to say to him. What if I say the wrong thing, and he never forgives me? And then maybe he gets mad and says something I can't forget?

"Well, what then? Did you have a fight with Cy or something?"

"No! I mean, sort of. It's Gary's fault. He's always hanging around with us now and . . . making everything weird."

Uncle Walt nods. "Because Gary likes you."

I shrug. "I guess so."

"And Cyrus likes Gary," Uncle Walt says.

My head swivels and I stare at him, then spit out the bite of bagel I'm never going to be able to swallow now. "How did you . . .? I didn't tell you that!"

"I've got eyes, Hitch, and nothing else to do but sit around here and watch everybody. That's an actor's job, you know. To figure out why people do what they do."

"You *can't* know! I promised Cyrus I wouldn't tell anybody!"

"You didn't tell me, and I won't tell anybody else. I'm just good at picking things up. The way Gary looks at you. The way Cyrus looks at Gary. It was kind of obvious."

I push my plate away. "Well, it wasn't obvious to me! Cy's been my best friend my whole life, and I didn't know this *big thing* about him. I feel like maybe I don't really know him at all. I mean, what else hasn't he told me?"

Uncle Walt reaches over and puts his hand on my head, which would annoy me if anybody else did it. "Maze, Cy probably didn't know either until recently. I'm guessing Gary is the first boy he's been attracted to. Or at least this is the first time Cy really understood what the attraction meant."

I can't look at those disgusting eggs or that greasy bagel another minute. I get up and take my plate into the kitchen and dump it all in the trash. Uncle Walt follows me.

"Are you upset because you hoped Cyrus would be your boyfriend?"

"No! You know we're not like that! I just don't want everything to change between us."

He leans against the sink while I slot my plate into the dishwasher. "Why should anything change?"

"Are you kidding? Everything is different now! He's . . . gay."

"Uh-huh." Uncle Walt pours himself another

cup of coffee. "I can see why that might be difficult for *him*—he has to decide how and when to come out to people, and I'm sure he's worried about that. But what does that have to do with you?"

I slam the dishwasher door closed. "It changes everything. You don't get it." I try to put my finger on the problem, but I can't quite explain it, even to myself. Cyrus likes Gary, who I'm just starting to like too. It's been hard for me to admit that, but for Cy to admit it is even a bigger leap than the one I'm making. And it feels like he's going someplace I can't follow.

"Look, Hitch," Uncle Walt says, "I know you're growing up in New Aztec, Illinois, which is not the most cosmopolitan place on earth, but it's not Brokeback Mountain either. Surely you know some other gay or lesbian people."

Well, sure, everybody knows the music teacher at school, Mr. Edwards, is gay, and most people are fine with that. And there's a woman Dad works with at the post office who's a lesbian, though I don't really know her. And, actually, there's a girl in fourth grade who has two fathers, but she lives on the other side of town.

"I guess I know a few people," I say, "but they aren't *my* age and they aren't my *best friend*."

"Are you the first person Cyrus has told?" Uncle Walt asks.

"Yeah."

"He hasn't told his parents?"

I shake my head.

"Well then, I guess Cy trusts you more than he trusts anybody else," Uncle Walt says. He gives me his crooked smile and starts to walk out of the room, then turns and looks back. "That's an honor, Maisie. Don't let your best friend down."

★22★

I'm glad I have to work on my history project today because it takes my mind off Cyrus and Gary and *the big secret*. Our computer is in the den, which is basically my room now, so there's nobody looking over my shoulder as I upload the footage to iMovie. I love going through the videos and seeing Grandma laughing and happy, especially after the scene yesterday at her condo. In the videos she mostly seems the same as ever, but I notice that every now and then a blank look comes over her face, like she's not at the kitchen table anymore, but in some other slightly out-of-focus place.

I listen to the interview about how she worked in her parents' grocery store and how Hank used to help her stock the shelves. I'm glad I kept the camera running for the rest of that story because I captured the look on her face when she told me about the dance at the lake. She has this little secret smile on her face, and it seems like she's watching it happen all over again, like a movie of it is playing in her head as she talks about it.

When I watch the footage a second time, I realize that when Grandma's talking about the past, she's completely at ease and happy, but when she gets pulled back into the present, her smile gets wobbly and she seems unsure of herself. Which is unbearably sad to watch.

Around noon there's a knock on my door, and Mom sticks her head in. "I'm back. Uncle Walt says you're working on your history project. How's it going?"

"Good," I say. "How's Grandma doing with Mary Jane?"

Mom sighs and comes into the room. "Well, it's not a match made in heaven. I guess Mary Jane didn't sleep much last night, because Grandma woke up at around three o'clock in the morning and decided she wanted to bake a cake."

"Bake a cake?"

"She didn't seem to know it was the middle of the night. And when Mary Jane tried to get her to go back to bed, Grandma threw a spatula at her and then a can opener. After that Mary Jane was afraid to go back to sleep. I made breakfast for both of them, and I think there's a truce in place."

I groan. "Doesn't sound good."

"I know. By the time I got there this morning, Grandma didn't remember anything about her middle-of-the-night shenanigans. Of course, the thing she *did* remember was that Hank was coming over today. Apparently he promised to bring her a pastrami sandwich for lunch from the deli near the theater." Mom leans against the wall as if she needs something to hold her upright. "I didn't even know she *liked* pastrami," she says. "Of course, I didn't know she liked *Hank* either."

"I guess she kept a few things secret," I say.

"Apparently. Where's your father? Bowling, as usual?"

"He went to Baldwinville to look at that truck."

"What? We can't afford a new truck!"

"He said it would be a big help when we have to move Grandma's things. We wouldn't have to hire a moving van."

"For the cost of that truck, we can hire a dozen moving vans!"

"Don't be mad at him. It's a used truck, not new." Mom and Dad don't fight very often, but I know from past experience that when money gets tight, they get on each other's nerves.

"I'm not mad at him, Maisie. I'm just frustrated. Used or not, we can't—"

She's interrupted by a buzzing phone and stomps off to dig it out of her purse. I hope it's not Dad saying he bought the truck. I'm waiting for the yelling to begin, but then I hear Mom say, "She *fell*? Is she okay?"

I go to the door so I can hear better. Uncle Walt is sitting in the living room, checking his phone, but he struggles to his feet and walks closer too.

"Well, where was Mary Jane?"

It's about Grandma, which is the other thing I was afraid of. Uncle Walt tilts his head back and stares up at the ceiling.

"Oh, for God's sake!" Mom grits her teeth. "I'll be there in ten minutes. And . . . thank you for calling me." She hangs up, stares at the phone for a minute, and then collapses in tears.

Uncle Walt goes over and puts his good arm around her so she can lean against him while she cries. "What happened?"

"I just left there half an hour ago and already—" Mom takes a deep breath and tries to stop herself from falling apart.

"Grandma fell?" I ask. "Is she hurt?"

"Who was that on the phone?" Uncle Walt wants to know.

"Hank Schmitz," Mom says. She pulls a wad of tissues from a box on the dining-room table. "When he showed up with his pastrami sandwiches, nobody answered the door. It was open, as usual—that's another thing that has to change—so he went in and found Ma lying on the kitchen floor, moaning. Apparently she spilled grease while she was trying to fry up some bacon, then slipped in it and hit her face on the table. He says that she cut her cheek and that one side of her face is already turning black and blue."

"Oh my God." Uncle Walt rubs his hand over his forehead like he's got a headache. "Why was she frying bacon?"

"Hank said she forgot she'd already had breakfast."

"Where was Mary Jane?" I ask.

"Sleeping," Mom says with a heavy dose of disgust.

Now Uncle Walt looks like he might cry too, but Mom has pulled herself together. "I have to get over there. And you're coming with me this time." She pokes a finger into Walt's chest. "I know you don't like to see her this way, but she's your mother too, and you're not in California for a change, so you're going to help me."

Uncle Walt nods, but he looks a little sick. "Yeah, okay. Let's go."

"I'm coming too," I say. "You might need me."

"Oh, Maisie, I don't know," Mom says. "Maybe you should stay here and work on your project."

But I'm already at the front door. There's no way I'm staying here. I wouldn't be able to think about anything else anyway. As we hurry out to the car, I can feel Cyrus's eyes on me from across the street, but I don't look over at him. Because everything is different now, and I can't pretend like it isn't. And I don't trust my eyes not to say the wrong thing.

★★

When we run into Grandma's place, she's sitting on the couch real close to Mr. Schmitz, and he's holding a bag of frozen peas against her cheek. Mary Jane is sitting in a chair across from them, her hands folded in her lap, her mouth all puckered up like she just ate a lemon.

Grandma looks pale and a little shaky, but as soon as she sees Uncle Walt, a smile breaks across her face. "Walter, you're home! I didn't know you were coming! When did you get here? Come give me a hug, sweetheart!"

Uncle Walt's face twitches, but he goes over and leans down to hug her. "Hi, Ma. Did you forget I was staying with Cindy for a while? I hurt myself, remember?" He points to the bandage beneath his shirt.

"Oh, no! How did that happen?" Grandma asks.

Mom interrupts her. "Walt is fine, Ma. It's you we're worried about. Let me see your cheek."

Mr. Schmitz lifts the bag of peas, and we see a red gash about an inch long under Grandma's right eye. The eye itself is swollen almost shut and turning an ugly purple color. It makes me dizzy to think how hard she must have hit the table to do that much damage.

"I cleaned it up as well as I could," Mr. Schmitz says. "There was antibiotic cream in the medicine cabinet, but I think she probably needs a couple of stitches."

"Oh, let's not make a big fuss," Grandma says. "Why don't we have some tea?"

"Do you want me to make it?" We all turn to look at Mary Jane, who we'd forgotten about.

Mom walks over and puts a hand on her shoulder. "Mary Jane," she says, "I'm not blaming you. I know you've had a hard time here, but—"

"I don't know how I could have fallen asleep," Mary Jane says. "I just lay down for a minute, and that foldout couch is like sleeping on rocks. Normally I'm a very light sleeper—"

"I'm sure you are," Mom says. "But I'm afraid this just isn't working out. You and my mother don't seem to be—"

"Oh, we'll figure it out," Mary Jane says. "Me and Evelyn will get to be great friends, won't we,

Evelyn?" She winks at Grandma, but Grandma won't even look at her.

All of a sudden Uncle Walt's face knots up, and it looks like he's going to spit at Mary Jane. "Do you even realize what's happened here? You were hired to make sure my mother didn't hurt herself, and yet she was *frying bacon* while you were fast asleep. We're lucky she only slipped in the grease. She could have burned herself, or caught the whole house on fire while you were snoring in the back room!"

I'm kind of shocked. Uncle Walt hardly ever raises his voice. It's hard to get him upset, but he's furious now.

Mary Jane sits up straight in her chair and glares back at him. "And just who are you?"

Mom steps between them. "This is my brother, Walter. I think what he's trying to say is—"

But Uncle Walt isn't going to let Mom soften the blow. "I'm not *trying* to say anything. I'm telling you, Mary Jane, you're *out*." He points his thumb at the front door. "You blew it. This job is over."

Mary Jane gets up. "Well, I'm not sorry to leave a work environment like this. I can find a better job than working for people like you." She heads for the back room, to get her stuff, I guess.

But Uncle Walt has the last word. "And don't ask us for any references!" he calls after her.

Mom looks kind of shocked. "Well, thank you, Walter. I guess that had to be done."

"It sure did," Hank says, with a grumbly laugh.

"I guess you told her, didn't you, Walter?" Grandma says. "I'm not the least bit sorry to see the back of that silly woman. I don't know why you hired her anyway, Cindy."

Mom slumps into the chair Mary Jane just got out of. While we wait for Mary Jane to throw her things into a bag and scuttle out the door, Grandma reaches out for Uncle Walt's hand and pulls him to her side.

"Hank, I don't think you've met my son yet," she says. "Isn't he a wonderful boy? And he's a very famous actor too!"

Hank reaches over and shakes Uncle Walt's hand. "Quite a family you've got here, Evie."

"Yes, it is," Grandma says. She looks up at Hank adoringly. "And I'm so glad you're a part of it now!"

Mom doesn't want me to sit around the emergency room with them while she and Uncle Walt wait for Grandma to get her stitches, so Mr. Schmitz offers to drive me home. Mom isn't sure about that either, but I pull her aside and whisper, "Don't worry. He doesn't even like me that much."

"Is that supposed to make me worry less?" she asks.

But in the end, I climb into Mr. Schmitz's old rust bucket. He doesn't drive fast, but every time he hits the brakes, they scream like they're in agony, and when he turns a corner, it sounds like the engine is going to fall out onto the street. He doesn't seem to notice, though. He doesn't seem to notice anything, including me.

"You need a new car," I say, just to remind him I'm sitting here.

"You need to mind your own business," he says. But then he gives this little laugh and shakes his head. "You're a pistol, you know that? Kind of like she used to be."

A *pistol*? Like in gun? What does that mean?

"Grandma used to be a pistol too?" I ask him.

"Oh, yeah. She didn't let you get away with anything. Always had an answer for everything. Just like you."

"I'm doing a history project about her," I say. "I interviewed her, and now I'm cutting the video into a short film."

"Oh, yeah?" He actually looks at me. "That's nice. Evie deserves a movie."

We're quiet for a minute, and then Mr. Schmitz says, "So that was your famous actor uncle, huh? Good-looking guy. Reminds me of your grandpa."

I'm kind of surprised by that and try to think back to what my grandpa looked like. I mostly remember the years he was sick with cancer and got very thin. But was he good-looking before that? It's hard to tell with people you're related to. A kid doesn't think about how her grandparents look, just whether they're nice to her. And he was, mostly, unless I made noise while he was watching a baseball game. Then he'd scoot me outside and slam the door.

"Did you know my grandpa?" I ask him.

He grunts. "Not really. I met him a few times. He loved Evie. I was glad to see that."

He could tell that just by looking? I sneak a sideways glance at Mr. Schmitz. Was he good-looking when he was young? Who knows? He's taller than Grandpa was, and he's still got all his hair, although it's white as flour now. He definitely looks better when he's not acting so grumpy, but the only times I've seen him look anything close to happy were when Grandma was around.

"She told me you danced with her once," I say. I don't intend to mention the kiss.

Mr. Schmitz nods. "Just one time," he says.

"She remembers it, though," I say.

"Me too." He takes a deep breath. "This is your street, isn't it? I turn right here?"

"Yeah. We're the white house at the end."

He cruises down the street and pulls into our driveway. "Okay," he says. "Go finish up that project. Do your grandma proud."

I want to answer him, but my eyes get stuck on Cyrus and Gary, straddling their bikes in Cy's driveway. For the first time in my life, I wish Cy didn't live across the street from me.

"Okay," I say. "Thanks for the ride."

I'm out the door and about to slam it shut when Mr. Schmitz says, "I always hoped I'd get another chance to dance with her." I don't know what to say, but then I decide he's not talking to me anyway, so I just close the door. He backs out of the driveway and leaves me standing there trying to figure out how to avoid Gary and Cy.

But there's no escape. Gary waves at me like a policeman directing traffic through an intersection. "Hey, Maisie, come over! Are you done with your project? You want to ride bikes with us?"

I can't just ignore him. Slowly I plod across the street. Cyrus gets busy adjusting something on his handlebars so he doesn't have to make eye contact with me. I admit I'm grateful.

"Sorry," I say. "There was an emergency with my grandma this afternoon, so I'm not finished with my project yet."

Cy looks up, his eyes big and round, but he doesn't say anything.

"What happened?" Gary asks.

"She fell and hit her head and had to go to the emergency room," I say.

Cyrus looks as sad as if it was *his* grandmother who hurt herself. That's just how he is. Still, he doesn't say anything. Maybe we aren't speaking to each other anymore. Or maybe he isn't talking to me until I talk to him first. But we can't talk now anyway, not in front of Gary.

"Oh, man!" Gary says. "That's terrible. Is she okay?"

"Yeah, she's fine. I think she's going to have to move in with us, though. Mom says she's not safe alone at her place anymore."

Gary nods and looks very serious. "Who was that old guy who drove you home?" he asks. "He looked familiar."

"Mr. Schmitz," Cyrus says. "From the Lincoln Theater." His voice sounds different—thin, older— or maybe I'm just surprised to hear it.

"Yeah," I say. "He's an old friend of my grandma's. He's . . . helping us."

"Did he talk to you in the car?" Cy asks quietly. I guess the weirdness of me getting out of Mr. Schmitz's car is overriding the weirdness of our last conversation.

"A little. It's kind of strange. I think he likes Grandma. I mean *like* likes her."

As soon as I say that, contagious embarrassment strikes again. Apparently all you have to do is mention that anybody likes anybody else—even if they're seventy years old—and all three of us get red-faced and flustered.

Once we start to look normal again, Gary says, "We ought to work on the screenplay, Maisie. Couldn't you do that for a little while and finish up your project later?"

"I thought you wanted to ride bikes," Cy says to Gary. He's back to pretending I'm not there.

"I do," Gary says. "I was just thinking if Maisie could stay, we could do some writing now and go for a bike ride later, when she goes home to work on her project."

I look at Cyrus to see what he thinks of this idea. It's not hard to tell. His eyes have turned into dark, muddy sinkholes in which he'd obviously like to drown me. Just a minute ago he seemed like the old Cyrus, my best friend worried about my grandma, but now his look says, *Get out of here, Maisie. You're ruining everything.*

"I can't," I blurt out. "Besides, I don't want to work on the screenplay anymore. You guys should write it by yourselves."

"What? No!" Gary looks like I've hit him in the jaw with a punch he didn't see coming. "Come on, Maisie, we should all do it together. That's the fun of it!"

There's a lump in my throat so big I can't swallow. "I changed my mind," I say. "I want to write a script by myself. It's too hard with three people." I back up and get ready to run. "Anyway, I have to go now."

"Maisie!" Gary yells, but he doesn't seem to know what to say after that. Or maybe he's self-conscious about saying anything else in front of Cyrus. I don't know. We've all obviously fallen into deep, sloppy puddles of humiliation and don't know how to pull ourselves out. The last thing I notice is that Cyrus's face has gotten softer, like he's not as mad as he was before. Then I dash home so I can get inside the house before I start crying like I just watched the end of *Toy Story 3*.

By the time Mom and Uncle Walt get back with Grandma, my project is finished. The hardest part was writing the essay because I tried to make Grandma sound like the fun person she was a couple of months ago when I started filming it, but I couldn't stop thinking about the helpless, confused person Mom just took to the hospital. Did things really change that fast, or did I just start noticing?

Everybody is too exhausted to make dinner, so we order pizza, and Dad goes to pick it up.

"I'm not even hungry," Grandma says, leaning her head back in our most comfortable chair. There's a big bandage beneath her eye, and half her face is covered with an ugly bruise.

"As soon as we eat, I'm going back home," she says. "I need a good night's sleep."

"Um, Mom, we were thinking . . . ," Uncle Walt says, and then looks at my mom for help.

"You're going to stay here tonight," Mom says. "You can sleep in the den. Maisie doesn't mind bringing her sleeping bag out here in the living room for a night . . . or two. Do you, Maze?"

"It'll be sort of like camping," I say, even though our lumpy couch is about as comfortable as a bag of bricks.

Grandma shakes her head. "Don't be ridiculous! Just because I got a little shiner? I'd rather sleep in my own bed."

"I know you would, but . . ." Mom looks at Uncle Walt.

It takes him a minute, but then he sits up straight and says, "I haven't gotten to see that much of you, Mom. Why don't you stay over here tonight? I'll make us all pancakes in the morning."

Grandma brightens. "You do make the best pancakes, honey. With strawberries?"

"Sure," Mom says, even though strawberries are a luxury we probably won't have very often now that she's out of work. "I'll call Dennis, and he can stop and pick some up after he gets the pizza."

"Maisie'll flip 'em for me, won't you, Hitchcock? So I don't toss flapjacks on the floor with my left hand." Uncle Walt winks at me, and I smile as though we're all having a great time making plans.

"Well, then," Grandma says. "Maybe I *will* stay over. I'm so tired."

When Dad gets back, we eat pizza in silence. Nobody says a word. It's really bizarre. As soon as we're done, Mom goes off with Grandma to help her get ready for bed, and Uncle Walt goes outside to answer a phone call.

I bring the plates and glasses in from the dining room, and Dad stacks them in the dishwasher.

"Been quite a day," he says.

I nod. "You didn't buy the truck, did you?"

"No. I just wanted to look at it." He grins at me. "Someday I'll get one."

I don't think he should count on that. With Mom not working and Grandma needing so much care, we probably won't be getting much new stuff for a while.

"I'm sorry you're being shuffled around so much, Maisie. It won't be forever."

"It's okay." I know Uncle Walt will leave when his collarbone is healed, but if Dad also means Grandma won't be around forever, I don't want to think about it.

"You're a good kid, Maze," he says. Then he lowers his voice and asks, "Want some ice cream?"

"You got ice cream?" That is definitely not on the out-of-work grocery list.

"When I stopped to get the strawberries, I saw there was a sale on this." He opens the freezer and pulls out a tub of mint chocolate chip. "I know it's extravagant, but I thought, under the circumstances, we all needed a little treat. It's not like I bought a truck, right?"

Mom comes in and flops in a kitchen chair. She watches Dad ladling out the ice cream, and I wait for her to start yelling at him. But all she says is, "Any chocolate sauce in the house?"

We squirt on chocolate sauce until the bottle is empty, and then stuff ourselves with ice cream like we're starving. We're half done with our big bowls by the time Uncle Walt comes back inside.

"Talking to your agent again?" Mom asks him.

Uncle Walt nods. "I called her this afternoon. There's been a change of plans, Cindy."

Mom looks at him, suspicious. "What do you mean 'a change of plans'?"

He walks in back of me and puts his hands on my shoulders. "I couldn't get the Skype audition, but Francine got me one in person. On Thursday. She said the casting agent sounded very positive about my chances."

"What are you talking about?" Mom says.

He sighs. "I'm leaving Wednesday."

"No!" I yell as I push my ice-cream dish away. What's left in the bowl isn't cold and delicious anymore. Now it's just lukewarm, melted soup, because obviously nothing good lasts forever.

Uncle Walt squeezes my shoulders, but he's looking at Mom, waiting for her to react.

Mom's eyes narrow into slits. Her hand grips the edge of the table, and for a minute I think she's going to throw her ice-cream bowl at him.

"You're leaving. Now. Just when I need you the most." A smile that looks like a storm warning lifts up one side of her mouth. "I don't know why I'm surprised. You've always run away from responsibility. Why should this be any different?"

Dad shakes his head, disgusted.

"Cindy, Dennis, just listen to me a minute. I knew you'd think that, but that's not what I'm doing. How much help am I being to you here, anyway? If I'm gone, Ma can move in here and Maisie won't have to sleep on the couch. And besides, what we really need is money. You won't be able to keep her here forever—that's not fair to you, or to Maisie either. Sooner or later, when this gets worse, she'll probably have to go into some kind of a home."

"Maybe not. You don't know that." Tears are running down Mom's face now. "I can take care of her! She's my mother, even if she likes you better!"

Dad scoots his chair over and pulls her head onto his shoulder. "Honey, let's just hear what Walt has to say, okay?"

Uncle Walt takes a deep breath. "Francine thinks I have a good chance of getting the part on this pilot, and she thinks the pilot has a good chance of being picked up. The showrunner has a great track record. I know nothing in Hollywood is a sure thing, but it's the best shot I've had in a long time. And if I get it, I can contribute real money. I'll put it aside for Ma's care. I swear to you, Cindy, I will."

Mom shakes her head and tries to stop crying, but she can't seem to. Nobody says anything for a minute, until finally I say, "Your collarbone isn't healed yet. Who'll take care of you in LA?" My voice sounds shaky, but so far I'm managing not to cry. Everything is so hard already; how am I going to get through it if Uncle Walt isn't here to help me?

Uncle Walt kneels down next to my chair and takes my hand. "I'll be okay, Maze. My ribs feel better now, and even if I can't drive right away, I can take taxis for a while. To tell you the truth, I probably could have stayed in LA and figured out how to get by. But I guess your mom's right. When things aren't working out for me, I run away. And this time I just wanted to come home. I needed a dose of my buddy Hitchcock to fix me up."

His eyes look sparkly. I don't want him to cry, so I throw my arms around his neck. Which it turns out *makes* him cry, because, duh, he's still got a broken collarbone.

"I want you to stay longer," I tell him. "I'll miss you!" I feel so bad, I can't even think of a film to compare it to. Well, maybe something really tragic, like *Rebel Without a Cause*.

"I'll miss you too, Hitch. Tell you what. Save Tuesday night for me. We'll stay up late and have a movie marathon with lots of buttered popcorn."

I nod because I can't really talk anymore. I'm waiting for Mom to say, "Tuesday is a school night. Maisie can't stay up and watch movies!" But instead she looks up at Uncle Walt with shining eyes and says, "I want to believe you, Walter, but . . ."

He gives her a sad smile that should, in my opinion, shatter box-office records. "Have a little faith in me, Cin," he says. "I won't let you down this time."

She stares at him for a minute and then says, "Okay. Go, then. Go back there and do what you love, Walter. Get famous for all of us."

Monday is bad. I skip breakfast because Mom and Uncle Walt are in the kitchen with Grandma, and I can hear her quietly crying. I guess they're telling her about Uncle Walt leaving and her having to live at our house now. I already did my crying last night, and I don't want to get all puffy-faced again before I go to school, so I yell good-bye and run out the front door.

I saw Cyrus ride off on his bike fifteen minutes ago, earlier than we ever leave for school. I guess he's avoiding me, which normally would make me feel terrible, but nothing is normal anymore. If he wasn't avoiding me, I'd be avoiding him.

At lunch I see Cy sitting with Gary about two seconds before Gary sees me. He starts waving at me, but I pretend I don't see him and head straight for a table full of girls from my English class. They look at me funny when I plunk down my tray.

"Where's Cyrus?" this girl Katherine asks me. She looks confused, like I've come to school undressed or barefoot or something. Like Cyrus is a part of me I don't leave home without. Which I guess is true. Katherine has known me since kindergarten, and she's probably never seen me without him.

I shrug, and they go back to their conversation about where they're going on their summer vacations. Florida, Minnesota, the Grand Canyon. They'd probably feel sorry for me if they knew, but I'm glad I'll be spending the summer at home, watching movies. The girls ignore me, and I'm happy to be ignored.

When the last bell rings, I race out the door and grab my bike from the rack. I'm half a block away when I hear Gary yelling my name. I don't stop pedaling, even though I feel like a creep for running away from him. What else can I do? I can't let him like me, and I can't like him back. He'll just have to think I'm a rotten human being.

When I get home, Mom, Grandma, and Uncle Walt are sitting silently in the living room, watching old episodes of *Everybody Loves Raymond*.

If you saw their faces, you'd have no idea the show was a comedy. I go into the den and wait for this day to be over.

★★

But Tuesday is worse.

Tuesday is the day Mr. Halters's two sixth-grade English classes are taking a field trip to the Saint Louis Art Museum—an hour on bumpy buses, everybody singing and yelling, and the chaperones telling us to be quiet or *else*. Which would be bad enough, but oh yeah, Cyrus and Gary are in the other class.

I'm not sure what art has to do with English, but everybody always does field trips the last few weeks of school, and sometimes the destination is kind of random. I like Mr. Halters. He's an easy-going teacher, and he looks a little like Cary Grant in *Bringing Up Baby*. When he wore the glasses.

Our class went to the art museum last year too. Cyrus and I had a great time that day. When we looked at paintings, we imagined what the movie would be if the painting was a poster for it. Like, there was a painting of a covered wagon and some mules crossing a prairie with blue mountains in the background, and we decided it was a poster for a sci-fi movie called *Happy Trails, Aliens*, directed by

★181★

Clint Eastwood, about a lonely old cowboy who gets lost in magical blue mountains inhabited by creatures from a crashed spaceship. We thought Harrison Ford could star, and Anne Hathaway would be perfect for the alien leader. (They would not fall in love.)

But today everything is different. Today I have to hide from Cyrus, who hates me, and from Gary, who likes me too much and ruined everything.

I keep to the back of the group when the classes are starting to get on the buses. I inch forward as I watch Cyrus and Gary, who are standing together and looking back and forth from one bus to the other. Looking, probably, for me.

I notice Katherine isn't talking to anybody, so I sneak over to her. "Hey, Katherine!"

She jumps. "Oh! Hi, Maisie. I didn't see you. Where's Cyrus?"

My smile falters. "Why do you always ask me that? He's not the only person I ever hang around with."

"He isn't?"

"No," I say. "Sometimes I like to be with girls."

"Oh. Okay." If Katherine was in a movie, she'd be the third-best friend of the main character, somebody who mostly stands quietly in the background and says, "Yeah, me too," like Joan Cusack in *Sixteen Candles*.

"Are you . . . Can I sit with you on the bus?" I ask her. I don't really want to. It's always been so easy to talk to Cyrus that I never bothered to figure out how to talk to people I don't know as well. An hour on the bus with Katherine will be work, but I need to have an explanation ready in case Gary finds me.

"You want to sit with *me*?" Katherine asks.

"That's what I just said!" Already she's starting to get on my nerves, but I don't know who else to ask. Most of the other girls I know have best friends they'll be sitting with, but as far as I can tell, Katherine is up for grabs.

She shrugs. "Okay." She doesn't seem any more enthusiastic about it than I am.

Just as we're getting on the bus, Gary spots me. "Maisie!" he yells as he runs over. "Cyrus and I have seats on the other bus. Come with us!"

I point at Katherine. "Sorry! I promised Kath I'd sit with her." *Kath?* I've never referred to her that way in the entire time I've known her. No one does. She turns and stares at me. I don't think she'd have been any more surprised if I opened my mouth and butterflies flew out.

I climb up the bus stairs, having managed to escape riding with Cy and Gary. Cyrus will be happy, even if Gary isn't. I guess this is how it's going to be from now on—I'll have to stay away from them. I miss Cyrus, though, even if he doesn't miss me.

It's a long ride. Katherine tells me all about the church camp she's going to for two weeks in August. Apparently she goes every year and they do a lot of praying and horseback riding. I don't know much about either of those things, so I just say "uh-huh" a lot until she gets tired of talking to a robot and looks out the window. I guess I was lucky that Cyrus wanted to be my friend all these years, because I don't seem to know how to make any others.

The museum is okay. Katherine walks around with the same group of girls she had lunch with yesterday, and I tag along with them as if that's not weird at all. Four out of five of them are wearing shorts and tank tops, and the other one, Esther, is in a dress so tiny that her hair is actually longer than her skirt. In my jeans and T-shirt, I look like their little sister.

Gary has figured out that something is wrong. He's stopped begging me to join him and Cyrus, but he keeps staring at me until I'm so self-conscious that I feel like *I'm* in a movie. Like I'm acting in a silent film and everything I do is exaggerated so my audience (Gary) understands it. *Look at us girls appreciating these Van Goghs!* [Mouth open in awe.] *But this Picasso is dark and depressing—we're not sure how we feel about that.* [Eyebrows scrunched together.] *Oh, my herd is moving to the next room now. I must hurry so I don't lose them, these girls I barely know.* [Big smile to show how much I'm enjoying myself with my new skimpily dressed pals.]

I like looking at the paintings, but it's a long, nerve-racking morning, and I'm grateful when we get back on the bus. To my relief, the chaperones announce we should take the same seats we had before. Katherine doesn't look too thrilled. It occurs to me that if I'm going to find a girl to be friends with, I should probably look for somebody who actually likes me.

Our second stop is the Gateway Arch, that enormous silver croquet hoop that looms over the Mississippi River as you cross into St. Louis from the Illinois side. We've all brought bag lunches that we're supposed to eat on the grassy lawn outside before we get into the tram cars that take us up to the top of the Arch.

I'm tired of pretending I want to hang out with Katherine and her friends, so I check where Cyrus and Gary are sitting, then choose a spot where I can be far away from them and alone. But my peanut-butter sandwich sticks in my throat. I can't help it—I miss Cyrus. I even miss Gary, but I *really* miss Cyrus. We haven't spoken in three days, which hasn't happened in the entire history of our friendship.

I don't care if Cy is gay as long as I can still be his best friend. Why didn't I say that to him right away? But maybe he doesn't want a girl best friend anymore. Maybe he wants Gary to be his boyfriend *and* his best friend. Probably he wants me to disappear so Gary won't like me more than him. But then I wouldn't have either one of them, my old friend or my new one. How is that fair?

A group of boys from the other class is sitting a few feet away, but they aren't paying attention to me. They're talking about the Andy Warhol exhibit we just saw at the museum, which was mostly portraits of famous people—Marilyn Monroe, Michael Jackson, Elizabeth Taylor—in bright, garish colors.

A kid named Tyler says, "I heard one of those paintings is worth millions of dollars. I don't get it. They don't seem that great to me."

Another boy, Chris, laughs. "Like you know anything about art."

"I know something about Andy Warhol," Tyler says. "I heard he was gay."

The boys' ears perk up then, and mine do too. One of them says, "He was a homo?"

"All those artists are homos," Chris says, like he's an art expert.

"Ugh," one of the guys says. "Why do they make us go and see stuff like that? I don't want to see a bunch of gay art."

I don't even know I'm going to say it, but I turn around and all of a sudden I'm yelling at them. "God, do you have one working brain cell among the four of you? You don't even know what you're talking about! For one thing, not all artists are gay, and for another, so what if they were? The important thing is the paintings, not whether the painter is straight or gay . . . or anything else, for that matter!"

The boys are all staring at me, and so are a bunch of other kids. I guess my voice carries.

"How do you know so much about it?" Chris says. "I guess you must be a lesbian, huh?" They all crack up then, rolling around on the grass and hooting like demented owls.

I can feel how red my face is, and I wonder if people think I'm blushing because it's true—that they think I *am* a lesbian. I don't care what those dumb boys think, but a lot of people overheard them. I don't look around, but I know kids nearby are watching me.

I crush my paper bag and stand up. I can't just walk away without saying anything, but everything I think of seems wrong. Finally I just say, "Grow up!" and that makes them howl even louder.

I throw my bag in the trash and find Mr. Halters. "I don't feel good," I tell him. "Can I just wait on the bus?" He nods and doesn't even ask me what's wrong. He probably thinks I have my period or something, which is also embarrassing since I'm probably the only girl in my class who hasn't gotten it yet. I climb into the hot, yellow box, and I'm relieved to see that the driver is fast asleep in his seat. At least I won't have to deal with any comments from him.

I'm sorry to miss going to the top of the Arch, but I've been up there before. Grandma likes to go because she remembers watching it being built. (At least she used to remember that.) From the top you can see across the whole city, but it's a little scary too. In the brochure we got it says the Arch is 630 feet high and was built to sway in the wind so it won't break. When you're up there, it makes you dizzy to think how high you are, swinging around like that.

I'm dizzy enough as it is. Not because of what those miserable kids said to me. I don't think I'm gay because . . . well, because I like Gary Hackett even though I'm trying not to. But Cyrus probably *is* gay, and it's pretty obvious some kids would be mean to him if they knew. Cy wasn't just afraid of telling me—he was afraid of telling anybody, of letting the truth out into the world. I get that. Just knowing that I know his secret must make him feel like he's 630 feet in the air, swaying back and forth with nothing underneath him.

★26★

I have to sit by Katherine again on the ride home, but I get the window seat this time, so I can lean against the glass and pretend I'm sleepy. Nobody says anything to me about the lesbian crack, but I know they're all talking about it. That kind of thing circulates through a sixth-grade class like pee in a swimming pool.

Our bus gets stuck in traffic, so we get back later than the first bus, and Gary and Cyrus have already gone home. Which is fine. I don't know yet what I'm going to say to Cy, and besides, I can't say it in front of Gary.

When I get home, I call Cy's house and his mom answers. "He's not here, Maisie," she says. "He's over at Gary's. I just assumed you were with them."

"Oh, right," I lie. "I forgot we were going over there today." No reason to make her suspicious.

I get myself a glass of iced tea and walk out the back door. Grandma and Mr. Schmitz are sitting side by side in patio chairs, holding hands. It was weird enough to see this going on at Grandma's house, but now it's happening in my *own* house. I'm not freaked out about it because they're old; I'm freaked out because they're not in the least embarrassed. They really like each other, and they're just sitting out here, letting everybody see it. I don't know where people get so much nerve.

I'm just about to turn around and go back inside when Grandma says, "Sit down, Maisie," and because I'm glad she knows who I am, I do.

"Where's your boyfriend?" Mr. Schmitz asks.

Oh, for Pete's sake. "I told you, Cyrus is just my friend," I say, but then I'm not sure that's true anymore.

Mr. Schmitz nods. "Right. You told me."

"Aren't you ever at the Lincoln anymore?" I ask him.

He grunts. "I'm there as much as I need to be. Besides, it's about time I retired, don't you think? "

"You wouldn't close it, would you?" I ask. That would be about the worst thing to ever happen in New Aztec.

Grandma stares at her fingers, all knotted up with Mr. Schmitz's, and doesn't pay the least bit of attention to our conversation.

"Nah, I'll get somebody to run it for me. Too bad you're not old enough. Oh, I forgot, you're moving out to Hollywood, aren't you?"

"I hope so," I say. I'm trying to imagine the Lincoln Theater without ·Mr. Schmitz prowling around it. "If you retire, can you still go there and watch movies for free?"

He laughs a little. "I think I've seen enough movies for one lifetime."

I don't see how that could be true. "What's on this weekend?" I ask him.

"Not sure. Check the newspaper," he says.

"You don't *know*?" I can't even believe this.

"Kiddo, there are other important things now." He winks at Grandma, and her face gets all soft and sweet.

"Okay, well, I have homework," I say, so I can go inside and escape whatever is happening out here on the patio. There's no homework on a field-trip day and not much left to do for next week either. And then school's out for the summer. I always spend the summer hanging out with Cyrus, going to movies and talking about movies, and this summer we were supposed to be making a movie. If Gary Hackett hadn't started hanging around us, that's what we would be doing.

While I'm finishing my iced tea in the kitchen, I look out the window and see Mr. Schmitz stand up and put out a hand to Grandma. I can't hear what they're saying, but she's laughing. She stands up, and Mr. Schmitz puts a hand around her waist and . . . they *dance*. There's no music, and they're waltzing around on a cracked-cement patio on a ninety-degree afternoon, but they don't seem to care about any of that.

I get goose bumps watching them. Mr. Schmitz's wish has come true. He's gotten another dance with Evie.

When I go into the living room to give them their privacy, I hear grunting and groaning coming from the den—or rather, my room. Or for now, Grandma's room. I don't know what we're calling it these days.

"Oh, good, Maisie's here," Mom says. "Can you help push? Uncle Walt only has one good arm."

I stand next to Uncle Walt and brace my shoulder against the instrument. "Where are we moving it?"

"Into the living room," Mom says. "It'll be tight in there, but I can't bear to part with it."

"And I won't let her," Uncle Walt says.

"Listen, if I wanted to, you couldn't stop me," Mom says. Sometimes I think the two of them enjoy their arguments.

"On my count," Walt says. "One, two, three, *push!*"

The piano moves half a foot. But we do it again, and it moves another half a foot. Little by little, six inches at a time, we get it through the den door, into the living room, and up against the living-room wall. Coming through the front door, you practically bump into it, but we move the couch forward a little so there's just enough space to walk through the room.

"It fits," I say.

"Barely," Mom says, looking doubtful.

"Barely is good enough," Uncle Walt says. "Besides, now you can't hide away when you play. You have to be on stage."

"Yeah. Everybody will love that, I'm sure."

"Play something now, Mom," I say.

She puts up her hands in protest, but Uncle Walt insists too, and finally she sits on the bench and starts to play a medley of Cole Porter songs, starting with "Anything Goes" and then sliding into "Let's Misbehave." Pretty soon Uncle Walt and I start singing along with Mom, and before you know it, Grandma and Mr. Schmitz dance right into the living room.

"Now we're cookin'!" Mr. Schmitz says. He twirls Grandma around, and her dress swings from side to side.

It's so much fun to watch them circle and turn, their steps matching perfectly. I let myself forget for a few minutes that Uncle Walt will be leaving tomorrow, that Cyrus is mad at me, and that Grandma has a better memory of what happened fifty years ago than what happened yesterday.

Uncle Walt and I start our movie marathon at eight o'clock. Mom lays down the law, telling me I have to be in bed by midnight, so the marathon is really only two movies: *Dead Poets Society*, my choice because I'm feeling lousy anyway so let's just dig in deeper, and *Tootsie*, Uncle Walt's choice because it's funny and for some reason he thinks I need cheering up.

I'm a little teary at the end of *Dead Poets* because Robin Williams was the best teacher ever and it wasn't his fault the kid killed himself, and then when all the boys climb up on their desks to salute him—well, it slays me. And I wonder why people can't understand each other better. Why do they hurt each other all the time, even when they don't mean to? Which makes me think of Cyrus, which makes me have to get the tissue box from the bathroom.

I've never seen *Tootsie* before, so Uncle Walt launches into a big introduction. "Dustin Hoffman wanted to make this movie because the greatest challenge for an actor is to play the other gender. It took four makeup artists to figure out how to make him look realistically like a woman. Dustin said he wouldn't do it if—"

I interrupt him. "You don't actually know Dustin Hoffman, do you?"

"No, no. This stuff is just legend."

"Uh-huh. Could we just watch the movie?" Even though normally I love hearing all the inside info that Uncle Walt knows, tonight I just want to drown myself in other people's stories and forget about my own.

Uncle Walt is right. *Tootsie* is hilarious. Every single actor seems perfectly cast, and the scene where Dustin Hoffman takes off his wig and announces on live TV that he's not really a woman has me choking on my popcorn.

As soon as the credits start to roll, Uncle Walt goes to the kitchen for another beer. He calls back to me, "Was I right? Was that a satisfying ending, or what?"

I agree it was. "But at the end of a movie, don't you always wonder what happened *the next day*?"

Uncle Walt laughs as he sits back down next to me on the couch. "That's the great thing about movies, Hitch. The end is the end; everything is resolved one way or the other. You feel joyful or peaceful or relieved, or sometimes disturbed or depressed. But if it's a good ending, it satisfies you, even if it's sad. The war is over, the guy gets the girl, whatever. Real life is a whole lot messier. It doesn't end when things are at a good stopping point."

"Yeah," I say. "You don't see the part where another war starts or the girl dumps the guy."

"I admit I'm partial to the ones with happy endings," Uncle Walt says. "What can I say? I'm an optimist. I like to believe the happy ending lasts forever."

"I guess it's hard for me to believe that," I say. The sorrow I've been holding off for the past few hours begins creeping over me again. "I don't want you to leave tomorrow. If you stay, we could do this all the time. You could teach me all the stuff I need to know."

Uncle Walt puts his hand on my head. "Hitchcock, you already know more about movies than any twelve-year-old I ever met. Be patient. You'll grow up soon enough."

I pull away from him a little bit. "That's not what I'm talking about. I don't even want to grow up."

"Of course you do. Don't be silly. Hey, you're not whining, are you?" Uncle Walt starts throwing popcorn kernels at my ear. "There's no whining in baseball!"

Which makes me half smile because that's a takeoff on the best line from *A League of Their Own*, which is probably one of my top twenty movies ever. I put a few of the kernels that fell in my lap into my mouth.

"Since when do you not want to grow up?" Uncle Walt says. "You're making such great progress at it."

I shrug. "Since now. Since being twelve. I don't want to be a teenager."

"Well, you can pause a movie, Maisie, but you can't stop time." Uncle Walt is silent for a minute, and then he says, "I'm guessing this Peter Pan attitude has something to do with Gary and Cyrus."

Since he already knows a lot of what's been going on, I decide to go ahead and tell him about what happened at the Arch this afternoon. It's my last chance to get some advice from him before he disappears back to California, so I might as well take advantage of it.

When I'm done, he shakes his head. "I'm sorry that happened to you, Maze. You're right—twelve is hard. Did anybody make fun of you afterward?"

"No, but I don't care if they do. It's not like

'lesbian' is some terrible insult. It's just annoying that they *think* it is."

"See, you're practically grown up already," he says, smiling.

"But I'm afraid if Cyrus tells Gary how he feels and Gary tells other kids, people will say awful things to him, and it will hurt him more because he *is* gay." I remember the terrified look on Cyrus's face when he told me he liked Gary, and my eyes fill with tears. "I'm just as bad as those obnoxious boys! I'm Cy's best friend, and even *I* didn't say the right thing when he told me. I *still* don't know what to say." And then the crying is unstoppable.

Uncle Walt scoots close and puts his good arm around me. "We all make mistakes, Hitch. You were surprised and you got a little panicked, but you can make it up to him. If Cy ever needed a best friend, he needs one now."

"I know," I say, sniffling. "I'll make it up to him. But what if he tells Gary—"

"Your grandma used to say, 'Don't borrow trouble.' Maybe it will all turn out fine. Have you ever seen Gary be mean?"

"No."

"Well then, let's assume he won't be in this case either. And if he is, you'll be standing right there by Cyrus's side."

I hope Uncle Walt is right, but I'm still worried. The three of us are so mixed up together now. How can that ever work out?

And then I realize what I have to do. It's obvious. I have no other choice; I have to make Gary *not* like me. Not like me at all.

Apparently I cried so much last night that I don't have any tears left today for saying good-bye to Uncle Walt. I give him a hug while he's putting the last few T-shirts in his bag.

"Don't worry, Hitch," he says. "Everything will be okay."

I nod, but I take into consideration that Uncle Walt is an optimist. He believes in happy endings more than I do. "When will you be back?"

"I'm not sure. But if your mom needs me to come back and help her, I will."

"What if I need you?"

He bends over and kisses the top of my head. "Sweetheart, I'll do the best I can."

It's pouring rain, and Mom offers to drive me and Cyrus to school so we don't get soaking wet. I glance up at him when he gets into the backseat, but he doesn't look at me. How could I have let this happen? Just because Cy is a little different than I thought he was, how could I forget that he's still one of my favorite people on earth? Nobody gets me like Cy does. If Cyrus isn't my best friend anymore, I'll curl up in my dark little den—or whatever room I end up getting stuck in—and die of loneliness. I have to fix this, and I will as soon as my mother isn't sitting two feet away. Fortunately she has enough problems of her own these days and doesn't seem to notice that Cy and I aren't speaking to each other.

At school we're all herded into the gym, since the weather is too lousy for us to wait outside for the bell. Cyrus starts to walk away from me the minute we get inside, but I grab his arm and pull him into a corner. There's so much noise in that big, echoing room that I'm pretty sure no one will be able to hear us.

"I'm sorry I didn't want to talk about what you told me, Cy. I was surprised at first and a little mad that you were keeping a secret from me. But I get it now, why you didn't want anyone to know. I'm sorry I was such a lousy friend."

At first Cyrus just stares at the floor. "It's okay," he says.

"No, it's not okay. You're my best friend, and

you always will be. You should be able to tell me anything."

"I don't think we can be best friends anymore, Maisie." When he looks at me, I can see the hurt in his eyes. I hate that I put it there.

"Of course we can. Don't say that, Cy! You're the only best friend I want! Ever!" I guess I said that pretty loudly. A bunch of eighth-grade girls narrow their eyes at me and curl their lipsticked lips.

"What about Gary?" Cyrus says softly, his voice quivering.

I'm quiet for a second. "Sometimes I wish Gary would just disappear. Everything was fine before he showed up."

A smile flickers over Cy's face. "You don't wish that, and neither do I."

"Well, I *wish* I wished it," I say.

Cyrus clears his throat. "I heard what happened yesterday at the Arch. I guess that was my fault, huh? I mean, you were sort of defending me."

"Don't be silly. Those boys were being idiots."

"Anyway, thanks for, you know, sticking up for me and Andy Warhol. I'm sorry they said that stuff."

I shrug. "It doesn't matter."

"Gary was mad when he heard about it. He told me he still likes you."

I sigh and slump against the wall. "I'm sorry, Cy. I don't know how to make him stop."

"Do you want him to stop?" Cy asks. "It seems to me you like him back now."

I don't know what to say. I don't want to lie to Cyrus, but I have to put an end to this thing with Gary, whatever it is. And I have to stop hurting Cy's feelings.

"I don't like him that much," I say, willing it to be true. "I mean, Gary's nice and all, but not as a boyfriend. Not for me."

Cy nods. "Yeah, probably not for me either."

"How do you know? He doesn't even know you like him. Maybe if he *knew*—"

Cyrus interrupts me by leaning in and giving me a quick hug. "I can't, but thanks, Maze," he says, and then he scuttles off into the crowd before I can stop him. I guess that means he's not mad at me anymore, which is great, but I know everything is still not quite right.

At lunch I see them, Cyrus and Gary, sitting together near the windows. I have no intention of going over to them, but I'm standing there so long, looking for some other table I can possibly join (one that doesn't have Katherine sitting at it), that Gary comes up to me and lays his hand lightly on my arm. I wonder if he can feel the shiver race all the way up to my shoulder and down my back.

"We're over there," he says. "Come sit with us. Please?"

I seem to be powerless to refuse. In a daze, I follow him to the table. He's wearing a dark red shirt, not a T-shirt but a button-down shirt with the long sleeves rolled up to his elbows. I don't know why, but this makes me want to run my hand over the uncovered skin of his arm. Why did this happen to me when I didn't even want it to? My heart is hammering away, and I'm pretty sure I won't be able to swallow my food if I sit with them, but then Cyrus probably won't be able to either.

After we sit down, Gary says, "I wanted to tell you I talked to those guys, Chris and Tyler, about what happened at the Arch yesterday. I told them they were really out of line to say what they did. I said they should apologize to you, but I don't think they will."

He *did* that? "Oh, thanks," I say, trying to sound like the whole thing is no big deal. "You didn't need to. I mean, they're just jerks."

"You were totally right to yell at them," Gary continues. "When my cousin Max came out last year, some guys in his class made fun of him, and he got really depressed at first. I don't know why people get so crazy about whether you're gay or straight. Max is just a regular sixteen-year-old guy who has a boyfriend instead of a girlfriend."

Cyrus and I lock eyes across the table. I hope my eyes say, *See, what did I tell you? He's not going to freak out about this!* Even though I know that if the two of them become a couple, it'll be ridiculously hard to pretend I don't care.

"I was thinking maybe the three of us could do something after school today," Gary says. "It's stopped raining—we could ride our bikes up to Dairy Heaven or something."

I would *love* to do that. "No, sorry, I can't." I say it fast to make sure I get it out, to make sure the truth doesn't slip out instead. The truth that I want to spend as much time with Gary as I possibly can.

"You don't have homework, do you?" Gary asks. "Our teachers aren't giving much—"

"No, it's my grandma. I'm supposed to help my mom move her into my bedroom. We have to pack up her condo and—"

Gary's eyes brighten. "Cy and I could help, couldn't we, Cy?"

"I guess." Cy's voice is so quiet, I can hardly hear him. I don't look at him, but I know what I'd see in his eyes if I did. Disappointment that Gary wants to be with me.

"I don't think so," I say. "It's a small house. It won't take us that long."

"Even a small house has lots of stuff in it. When my grandpa moved—"

"Look, Gary, my grandma is very . . . private.

★207★

She doesn't want a lot of people going through her stuff."

"We won't go through it. We'll just help pack—"

"I said *no!*" I don't mean to sound so angry, but he won't give up and it's hard to keep saying no when I want to say yes.

Gary gets quiet then. "Sorry, Maisie. I guess I'm an idiot too." He looks out the window as if there's something a lot more pleasant than me out there.

Cy gives me a little kick under the table, and when I glance at him, his cloudy eyes say, *Thank you* and *I'm sorry*.

"I didn't mean to yell at you, Gary," I say. But I can't tell him what I did mean. "The thing is . . . I just can't . . . ." I want to say something to make him feel better, but I can't afford to make him feel better. I stand up and grab my tray full of uneaten lunch. "I just remembered I need to go to the library," I say. And then I slalom through the tables to make a fast getaway, no looking back.

I hate that I have to hurt either Cy or Gary. I don't want to hurt anybody, including myself. But it has to be one or the other because we can't all have what we want. Maybe none of us can.

Gary is right about how long it'll take to go through Grandma's condo and pack things up. Mom and Grandma and even Mr. Schmitz work at it for days, and I go over to help after school. Grandma wants to keep tons of stuff that we don't have room for in our house, so Mom ends up renting a small storage unit. We borrow a pickup truck from Dad's friend Jack and drag box after box of dishes and papers and tablecloths and who-knows-what-all down to the storage space.

On Friday afternoon Grandma points to a tall standing lamp that leans to one side and wears a ripped shade. "That lamp," she says. "I want to keep that."

Mom sighs deeply, which she does just about every time Grandma opens her mouth these days.

"You aren't going to need it at our house, Ma. And besides, we don't have room for it."

"We'll put it in the storage unit," Grandma says, as if that settles that.

"That space is practically filled up already," Mom says.

"Well, we should have gotten a bigger one, then! I told you that!"

It seems as if Grandma gets upset about more stuff on the days Mr. Schmitz isn't here. He can keep her calm better than anybody else.

Mom mashes her lips together as if she's keeping an angry reply inside. I know the storage unit is expensive, even the small one. Finally she says, "Fine. We'll keep the lamp."

"And my couch too," Grandma says.

Oops. Last straw.

"We cannot keep the couch!" Mom yells. "I told you, someone is coming from the consignment shop tomorrow to look at the furniture."

I keep wrapping stained napkins around mismatched silverware. I know already it doesn't help if I get into the conversation. But then Grandma starts to cry, and I can't pretend anymore that I'm just helping with normal chores. Nope. I'm packing up my grandmother's whole life so it can be hidden away in a small, windowless room. And that's just the stuff we aren't getting rid of altogether.

Grandma slumps into a kitchen chair. "Why are we doing this?" she says, tears streaming down her face. "I don't want to live at your house, Cindy. I want to keep my things!"

Mom puts down the roll of packing tape and kneels next to her mother's chair. She's had to explain this half a dozen times already, and I can tell it isn't getting easier. "You're forgetting things," she says quietly. "You need to live with us now, Ma. We can take care of you."

"I can take care of myself!" Grandma says, but I don't think she really believes it anymore. Now it's just what she wants to be true.

We give up on packing for the day and go home. It makes Grandma happy to cook for us, and she can still do that, as long as Mom stays with her to make sure she doesn't forget what she's doing and put salt in the soup three times or let the chicken burn in the frying pan. Sometimes she asks where my grandpa is, and sometimes she asks where Uncle Walt is. Mom and I both hate having to tell her they're not here, but somebody has to answer her questions.

When Dad gets home from work, he puts his arm around Mom and kisses her forehead. She slumps against him. None of us talk much, because what is there to say?

We're starting to appreciate the nights when

Mr. Schmitz comes for dinner. Grandma doesn't ask about the people who are missing when he's around. And he's not nearly as crabby as he used to be either—when he helps me clear the table and load the dishwasher, we sometimes talk about movies and he hardly growls at all.

The other night I asked him why he never showed *Frankenstein* at the Lincoln. "It's the best horror movie," I said, "but I've only ever seen it on DVD."

He shook his head. "Well, you won't see it at the Lincoln as long as I'm scheduling the shows."

"Why not? You don't like it?"

He sighed and put down the dish he had in his hand. "I think it's brilliant, but I can't bear to watch it again. It's the saddest movie I've ever seen."

Huh. It's true you feel bad for the monster. He doesn't mean to kill the little girl.

"I guess it's pretty sad," I said, "but I don't know how else it could have ended. I mean, a monster isn't going to get a happy ending."

"Why not?" Mr. Schmitz asks. "He's had such a hard time already. Why can't a monster have a happy ending? That's the movie I'd like to see!"

And I realized I'd like to see that movie too. It's cool the way Mr. Schmitz makes me see things a little differently than I usually do. Sometimes I think I almost *like* him now.

Tonight, as soon as dinner's over, I escape to the den, which is beginning to feel like my own space now. I've made it look more cheerful by tacking up some old yellow curtains from Grandma's condo over the brown wall paneling. The lamp Grandma didn't want to get rid of makes the room feel brighter too.

Mom knocks on my door and sticks her head in. "Phone," she says, holding it out to me.

I hope it's Cyrus, but I'm not really surprised that it's Gary.

"I've hardly seen you all week," he says.

"Yeah, sorry. I've been helping Mom pack up Grandma's stuff."

"Right," he says. "But it seems like you're avoiding me. I mean, me and Cy. Are you?"

"Avoiding you?" I say it as if that's the last possible thing I'd be doing. "I'm just busy right now is all."

"Okay," he says. "But you're not mad at me, are you?"

"*No!* Why would I be mad?"

"I don't know. Sometimes it seems like you are. You know, I really like hanging out with you, Maisie."

I swallow about eight times, but no words come out of my mouth. This is impossible. I can't let him hope I'm going to like him back, but I can't stand being mean to him either. Finally I manage to say, "Yeah, I know. The three of us are a great team."

He's quiet for a minute, and then he says, "We can all hang out this summer, right? The three of us, I mean? Your grandma will be all moved into your house and you'll have time, won't you? We can ride bikes and go to the pool and stuff."

I imagine what it would be like to go to the pool with Gary. He wouldn't be wearing a shirt, and I could look at his arms and his chest but pretend I wasn't. Maybe I could get a new swimsuit too— something less babyish than the racer-back I've worn for three years. Something that doesn't make me look completely flat-chested.

But then I come to my senses. Of course I can't get a new suit. There's no extra money for that kind of thing, and anyway, what's the point of looking . . . not-flat? I don't want Gary to see me in a swimsuit that covers less than my underwear does. He might think . . . whatever boys think. It's embarrassing just to imagine it, and I'm glad he can't see me blush.

"I guess we can hang out sometimes," I say. It comes out in a whisper, as if I don't actually want him to hear me.

"And go to the pool?" he asks again.

I consider hanging up right this minute so I

don't have to answer the question, but instead I say, "Maybe."

There's a quiet sigh on his end. "Good. Three more days of school, and then we're free for the summer. We'll have so much fun!"

"I guess we will," I say, not sure if I'm pretending to be enthusiastic or if I actually am. Then I make an excuse and hang up so I can try to figure out what part of me is telling the truth—my mouth or my brain or my heart.

It seems like ages since Cy and I have been to a movie on a Saturday by ourselves, but I guess it's only been a few weeks. Gary was really disappointed he had to go to a family wedding today instead of coming with us to see *Big*. I guess Cy is probably disappointed too, though he hasn't said anything. I'm not sure how I feel about it. I mean, the three of us together are kind of a disaster, but it feels wrong for Cyrus and me to walk into the Lincoln Theater without Gary, which is funny because we've come here without him a lot more than we ever did with him. But at least things are starting to feel normal between me and Cy again. I'm glad we'll have a few hours alone to try and get our friendship back on track.

There's some young guy I've never seen before behind the concession stand. I guess Mr. Schmitz is with Grandma today, or maybe he just decided he's tired of spending every Saturday afternoon vacuuming up popcorn kernels.

The crowd is bigger than usual, but we manage to get our favorite seats in the front row of the balcony. Cy buys a large buttered popcorn for us to share because he knows my mom isn't handing out much cash these days.

The part where Tom Hanks makes out with the older woman is a little awkward to watch with Cy sitting next to me. Thank God Gary isn't here. I guess I'm kind of like Tom Hanks's character. This woman really likes him, and he looks old enough to be her boyfriend, but he's really just a kid who's too young to know what to do about it.

The movie ends and the lights come on, but Cyrus and I are never the first ones out. We like to sit a minute with our feet up on the balcony railing and think about what we've seen.

"Tom Hanks is a cool grown-up at first, when he's acting like the kid he really is," Cy says. "But then he changes. When he gets used to being a grown-up, he turns into a jerk. That was kind of depressing."

I nod. "He forgot he was a kid. He got too serious about everything."

"Yeah. I hope that never happens to us."

"Me too," I say. "But maybe it happens even if

you don't want it to. Let's promise not to turn into completely different people than we are now."

"Pinky swear," Cyrus says. We hook our little fingers together like we've done a hundred times before, only this time I wonder if we're fooling ourselves. Maybe everybody changes when they grow up, and there's nothing you can do about it.

I'm not watching who's walking up the aisle down below us, but something catches my attention—maybe the blue dress. *Grandma's* blue dress—with Grandma in it! I lean over the railing to see. I guess I shouldn't be surprised that Mr. Schmitz is right beside her. I sock Cy on the shoulder and point down.

"Whoa!" he says. "Are they on a *date*?"

Do you call it a date when people are so old? Mr. Schmitz has his elbow out in a triangle, and Grandma is holding on to it. I can't hear what they're saying, but she smiles this enormous smile and looks up at him like she's looking at a rainbow.

And then Mr. Schmitz laughs. Laughs really loud. It's kind of shocking, as if somebody you've only ever seen in a wheelchair suddenly stands up and starts walking.

"I think they put a coin in a fortune-teller machine, like the kid in the movie," Cy whispers. "Only instead of asking to be big, they asked to be *young*."

He's so right, it makes me shiver.

We sit there a while until we figure Mr. Schmitz and Grandma have gotten into his car and driven off. The guy from the concession stand comes upstairs with a whisk broom, but he doesn't tell us to leave. He looks so sleepy, I'm not sure he even knows we're there.

We get on our bikes, but we're not ready to go home yet, so we ride to the park and sit on a bench. We're silent, but not because we don't want to talk. I think it's more because we're both trying to figure out how to say what we're thinking.

Finally I say, "Cy, do you think they *love* each other?"

Cyrus shrugs. "I never think of old people being in love. But that's kind of what it looked like, didn't it?"

"Can you tell by looking? At first I thought Mr. Schmitz was just an old friend who felt sorry for Grandma, but he comes over to our house all the time now, and last week they danced together."

Cy's eyes get big. "At your house? You saw them?"

"Yeah, we all saw them."

"Wow." Cy looks down at his sneakers as he kicks his heels into the dirt. "Have you ever thought you loved anybody? You know, besides your family."

I shake my head. "I'm not even sure what the word means. If you're talking about parents, sure, you love them, but sometimes you can hardly even stand them. So loving somebody your own age must be different than that, don't you think?"

Cy is quiet for a minute, and then he says, "Sometimes I think I love Gary."

On the one hand, I kind of knew he was going to say that, and on the other hand, I'm completely stunned to hear him say the words out loud.

"Are you sure?" I ask him.

"No," he says, "but that's how I feel when I'm around him. Is that how you feel too?"

"No, I don't," I say, and that's the truth. Although I think it might just be the truth *for now*, because I'm obviously a little bit behind Cyrus in figuring this stuff out.

Cy keeps pounding holes in the ground with his heels. "I guess the only thing that really matters, though, is whether Gary loves *you*."

I screw up my face. "Cy, aren't we too young to be talking about love? Isn't there some other word for when you like somebody a lot but you're only twelve?"

"I don't know what that word would be," he says.

I don't know either, but I don't intend to leap from friendship into love in a single bound. I don't think love is going to be my superpower, at least not until I'm older.

"You know what I think, Cy?" I look around to make sure there's nobody within hearing distance. "Maybe you have to tell Gary you're gay and see what he says. That's the only way to know for sure."

He shakes his head. "Maisie, you know I can't do that."

"I *don't* know that. You surprise me all the time. Like when you chased Buffy down the side- walk and caught her when Gary and I couldn't. And you're surprising me right now talking about loving people."

"Well, not just *any* people," he says.

"*Gary*. Saying you love Gary. You can do things I could never do! You have a secret strength, Cyrus."

Cy smiles and pounds his fist on my knee. "I wish that was true."

"It *is* true!"

He leans his head over so it just touches mine. Up until that moment I would have said Uncle Walt was the person I loved most in the world. (Not counting my parents, of course, but that's an ordinary kind of love.) But now I think Cyrus is in first place. Maybe it's not *love* love, but it's still kind of a big leap.

★31★

School is out, and Grandma is completely moved in. At night I sleep in the small den surrounded by ancient yellow curtains. Mom spends most of her time repeating things to Grandma and looking online for jobs she can do from home. Uncle Walt has been gone for more than a week and hasn't called once. He texted Mom that his plane landed, but that's the only thing I know. I miss him every day and almost wish he'd give up on Hollywood and move back to New Aztec. Almost, but not quite.

The only good thing that's happened in a while is that I got an A on my history project, the video about Grandma. When Mom and Dad watched it, Mom hugged me and said, "I'm glad we have this. Especially now," and Dad said, "I'm starting to think you might really turn out to be a filmmaker, Maisie!"

This afternoon is muggy, with thunderstorms predicted. Mom is taking Grandma to a doctor's appointment, so I ask Cy and Gary to come over to watch *Rear Window*. It's impossible to ignore Gary—he's always so nice to me. Besides, he doesn't know Cy's crazy about him, so if we don't include him he'll just think neither of us likes him anymore, and that doesn't seem fair.

Cy and Gary sit on opposite ends of the couch, with room left for me in the middle, but I sit on the chair instead. I can tell Gary is enjoying the movie, because he leans forward as if he's going to crawl into the TV.

When the credits come on, he says, "Wow, that was great! I think I liked it even better than *Psycho*. Now I want to watch all of Hitchcock's movies."

"We should do that this summer," Cy says.

Gary looks extremely pleased about the idea, probably because it nails down a plan for the three of us to spend a lot of time together the next few months.

"Do you think it was wrong of Jimmy Stewart to look into his neighbors' windows?" I ask.

"No," Cy says. "He caught a murderer!"

"Yeah," Gary says, "but he was looking at people for a while before he realized there was anything bad going on. He spied on people who were just living their normal lives too."

Cyrus thinks that over. "That's true. It was kind of weird at the beginning when he was sitting there staring at all his neighbors through binoculars."

"That's the genius of Hitchcock," I say. "He makes us feel uncomfortable watching Jimmy Stewart spy on people, but we can't stop watching either. It's fun to see people when they don't know you're looking at them. He makes us Peeping Toms too."

Cyrus has his socked feet propped on the coffee table and looks more confident than he has in a while. "So, is Stewart a hero at the end, or just a creepy guy who got lucky?" he asks.

"Both," Gary and I say simultaneously.

And then, because apparently even saying a word at the same time as Gary embarrasses me, I jump up and yell, "Anybody hungry?" and the three of us pad out to the kitchen.

There's no ice cream or Dr Pepper or tortilla chips in the house—they disappeared with Mom's paycheck—but there's plenty of cereal and milk.

We fill bowls and take them outside to the patio, where there's a little breeze beneath an overcast sky. The geraniums Mom planted last month look spindly and thirsty, but I'm pretty sure they'll get a drenching before the day is over.

Suddenly Cyrus says, "We should work on the script again."

Gary and I do *not* look at each other. "Really? All three of us?" I ask Cy.

He nods. "Yeah. It's summer. We need to make a movie."

Gary and I dare to smile at each other. "Okay," I say. "Can you bring over your mom's laptop?"

Cy puts his half-finished bowl on the table and heads for his house. "Back in a minute."

The second he disappears, I realize I'm sitting here alone with Gary. Neither of us knows what to say, so we just clank our spoons against bowls and teeth. Fortunately, our silence is almost immediately interrupted by a noisy argument that seems to be coming from my driveway. Car doors slam and I hear several voices, one of which is Mom's and one that sounds like Mr. Schmitz's. They're coming in the front door of the house, but we can hear them pretty well out on the patio with the back door open.

"But didn't you hear what *else* the doctor said?" That's Mr. Schmitz for sure. "It wasn't all bad news. Evie's short-term memory has been affected, but her long-term memory may be good for quite a while. She has good years left, Cindy. We want them to be happy years."

"We shouldn't have told her, Hank," Grandma says. "She treats me like a baby. We should have just done it and kept it to ourselves."

"Not tell me?" Mom says. "How was that going to work? You'd get secretly married and none of us would ever know?"

Married? Grandma and Mr. Schmitz are getting married?

"Cindy," Mr. Schmitz says softly, "try to understand. I've felt this way for a long time. Years. Now that I've found Evie again and she feels the same way, I want her to be my wife before it's too late."

I sneak up to the door and peek inside. Gary comes up behind me because obviously this is too good to miss. Mom is leaning against the refrigerator, staring at Grandma and Mr. Schmitz. Mr. Schmitz has his arm around Grandma, who's grinning like she just won the lottery.

Finally Mom says, "Where do you think you'll live? There's no room for you to move in here with my mother, Hank. She's in a small room and—"

"Of course not," Mr. Schmitz says. "We've talked about that. Evie will live with me at my place as long as she's comfortable there. I have plenty of room, and I can stay home to help her as much as I need to."

Grandma interrupts him. "And I can cook him good meals so he doesn't eat all those pastrami sandwiches."

Mr. Schmitz winks at Grandma, then turns

back to Mom. "When I do go to the theater, Evie can come with me. Or she can come here if you want, but this will free you up, Cindy. And if at some point down the line we—or you—think she'd be better off back here . . . or someplace else . . . well, we'll make that decision when we have to."

"I can't believe you came up with this whole scheme without even talking to me about it," Mom says. Her voice is shaky. "Do you really want to do this now, Hank? When my mother is so . . . compromised?"

Grandma's face tightens up. "Just because I can't remember every silly little thing doesn't mean my life is over," she says. "I never forgot Hank, did I? For God's sake, Cindy, the man moved back to New Aztec, Illinois, from New York City in the hopes that I was still available, and then I went and married somebody else. I think it's time I finally made good on that kiss I gave him fifty years ago."

Mr. Schmitz moved back to New Aztec for Grandma! He gave up making movies for her. It blows my mind that he sacrificed one thing he loved for the possibility of another. And she married my grandpa instead! At least it's working out in the end, but I wonder how long "the end" will last.

Hank steps forward and lays a hand on Mom's

arm. "It'll be good for all of us, Cindy. I love Evie. I love her with all my heart."

And then Mom starts to cry, and Grandma hugs her tight.

Gary and I tiptoe back to our patio chairs, where our cereal has turned to milky mush.

Cyrus comes running around the corner from his house, laptop in hand. "Did I miss anything?" he asks. I don't even know where to start.

We work on the script for the next week, either at my house or at Cy's. It's almost finished now, and we're going through it to figure out how and where to shoot scenes. We're sitting on the lawn in Gary's backyard with Buffy, trying to figure out how to include her in the movie with the least amount of hassle, when Cyrus's mom pulls up in her car.

"Let's go!" she yells out the window.

"Oh, right. I have a dentist appointment," Cy says. He gives Buffy's belly a last scratch and heads for the car. "I'll be back in an hour."

He's gone so quickly, I feel dizzy. Gary and I glance at each other, and then we both start busily petting the dog as though we're getting paid for it. Buffy is fast asleep and couldn't care less.

Gary clears his throat. "So, in that scene where

we knock on the door of the girl we don't like . . . what's her name again?"

"Kathy," I say. I've been thinking I'll ask Katherine to play this part—she'd be perfect.

"Right, Kathy. We could film that at my house so it's easy to have Buffy in it. She won't be able to get out of the yard."

I nod. "That could work. But I think the scene where we're running and chasing Buffy will have to be shot at my house because I have the biggest backyard."

"Okay," he agrees.

We both look down at Gary's giant buffalo dog, who's snoring and snuffling and whimpering all at the same time. I'm glad she's so noisy—it fills in the silences when we can't think of anything to say.

"I don't think we can count on Buffy to chase anything," Gary says. "She'll run if you don't want her to, but I don't think she'll do it on command."

"She'll run for treats," I say.

Gary laughs, but then there's a silence that Buffy fills with a deep groan as she flops her gigantic body from one side to the other. I'm determined to keep talking because I know once there's too much silence between us it will grow and spread like invisible kudzu until we're strangled into complete speechlessness. "Um, the other thing we need to decide is what the ghosts look like. I'm thinking a little scary, but not like vampires or zombies."

"I guess we'll wear white makeup," Gary says.

"With black around the eyes," I add.

"We should wear white clothes," he says. "Not sheets, though—that's stupid."

"Right," I say. "No sheets. Maybe we can powder our hair white."

"And powder Buffy's brown spots, so she's all white too," Gary adds.

"Too bad she's so big," I say. "It would be easier to powder a Chihuahua."

He nods but has nothing more to add. As I'm stroking Buffy's soft ears, I suddenly realize it's happening. The swampy silence is beginning to seep in around us. At first I'm only a little panicked, because I'm sure Gary will come up with something else to say—he's got to; it's his turn. But he doesn't. I'm a little sweaty now, and I search around for an obvious comment, something about the dog, about Katherine, about white faces . . . but nothing makes any sense. All the words in my brain have gone on strike.

And then, just to make matters worse, Gary scoots over close to me on the grass so I can just barely feel the hairs on his arm brushing against the hairs on mine. I stare straight ahead, totally paralyzed. Not even a finger moves.

"Maisie?" Gary says it so quietly I can hardly hear him, and still the word bounces off the walls of my skull. Why does my name sound so pretty when he says it?

"Mmmm?" It's not a word, but it's the only noise I'm able to make.

I can feel his hand cover my hand where it lies on the grass. "Would you be my girlfriend?" he whispers.

How can your worst nightmare also be your wildest dream? I look down at our hands. His is a little bigger than mine and very warm. I like seeing them together like that, surrounded by a carpet of green grass and breezy dandelions. It would make a nice shot in a movie. Except it's not a movie; it's real life.

"I can't," I say, my voice practically inaudible. "It's not a good idea."

"Why not?" I can hear his disappointment. "I really like you, Maisie. I asked Cyrus, and he said the two of you were just friends, so he wouldn't be jealous or anything."

Boy, is he wrong about that. I make a big mistake and look up into his eyes, which are dark and as deep as a river if you jumped into it from a high cliff.

"Unless you don't like me," he says. "But I kind of think you do."

Of *course* I do, but that's not the point. I don't say that to him, though. What I do say is, "I like you as a friend, Gary. Can't we just be that?"

He doesn't say anything for a long time, but our eyes are kind of stuck together, and I can't stop myself from jumping off the cliff. Finally he says, "Is that really what you want?"

And then he seems to be falling over, or I guess just leaning into me. I feel his hand brush up my arm until it grips my elbow and makes me quiver. He tilts his head to the side, and before I know it, his lips have fallen very softly against my lips. I just barely feel the thrill of it before he pulls away again. Wait . . . we *kissed*!

"Was that okay?" Gary asks.

I want to say, "It was great, but not quite long enough. Let's try it again." But of course I don't say that. Imagine if Cyrus saw us kissing? *Catastrophe.* So instead I say, "I don't think we should do that again."

I'm careful not to look at Gary while I tell this lie so I don't get stuck in his eyes again. He takes his hand off my arm, but the ghost of his touch is still there.

His mom bangs open the screen door, and we both jump. "Hey, you two. Aren't you hot out there in the sun?" she says. "Come in and have something to drink."

I wonder if Gary is as glad as I am for the interruption. What can either of us say next? We trudge inside, and his mother pours us glasses of iced tea. "Why don't you stay indoors for a while?" she says. "Watch a movie or something. Cool off."

Without a word I follow Gary into the TV room. His whole house is air-conditioned, and it's so cool that I shiver.

I try to scramble back to the time before the kiss, as if nothing has changed. "What should we watch? You know I'm not a *Star Wars* fan." I give a weak smile in the general direction of his head, but I don't see if he smiles back because I don't want to focus on his face that much.

"I know," Gary says. "I checked out some movies from the library. Do you want to watch *The Princess Bride*?"

"You checked out *The Princess Bride*?" I'm forced to look right at him to see if he's kidding or not.

He nods. "You were right. It's really good."

The fact that Gary not only got the DVD but watched it and liked it makes me wish even more that the kiss had been longer.

He puts the movie on, and we take seats on opposite ends of the couch. Once again Inigo Montoya seeks revenge for his father's death. Prince Humperdinck is still an evil liar. Miracle Max is as hilarious as ever. And Buttercup falls in love with

Westley, as she must. I've seen it a dozen times, but this time, sitting on the couch with Gary Hackett, seems like the first time all over again.

As much as I'm loving the movie, my brain is simultaneously repeating on a loop its own awesome film, entitled *First Kiss*. I can't stop thinking about it. Kissing Gary was not at all like kissing my own hand and pretending it was someone's lips, which I've only done once or twice, just to get an idea. Now I know what it *really* feels like. It's hard to describe, even to myself. Weird. Nice. Scary. Grown-up.

★33★

The movie is half over by the time Cy gets back. He looks a little surprised to see what we're watching, but I can tell he's glad we're sitting far apart. He plops himself down between us, just where he's supposed to be. I wonder if Gary will tell him what happened. I know *I* won't.

After the happy ending Cy says, "You know what this makes me think of? Your grandma and Mr. Schmitz. I mean, they're obviously a lot older than Westley and Buttercup, but still. They were separated for all those years, and now they're finally getting back together. It's pretty cool."

I nod. "Mr. Schmitz acts different now too. I actually like him."

"I guess being in love changed him," Gary says, his voice low and throaty. I can tell he's looking at me, but I'm carefully memorizing the pattern on the carpet. I can't believe he's talking about *love*, as if it's a normal topic of conversation. Even though I've watched people in movies fall in love a million times, to me love stories are as puzzling as murder mysteries. How does anybody have the guts to fall in love? Or to admit it to the other person?

Cyrus is sitting forward and bouncing his knee up and down as if he's nervous. I'm hoping he'll say something to change the subject, but then I get a glimpse of the look on his face—*pure fear*—and I'm pretty sure I know what subject he's about to bring up. I didn't see it coming, and I panic. "Maybe we should—" I begin, but it's too late. Cyrus has geared himself up, and he can't stop now.

"I have to tell you something, Gary," he blurts out. "Maisie knows already, but if we're friends, you should know too, so I'm just going to say it."

Why did I encourage him to do this? If Gary has a bad reaction, Cy could be really hurt!

"Cy," I say, "maybe this isn't the best time to—"

"Yeah, it is, Maze," Cyrus says. "I'm tired of keeping it a secret."

Gary looks a little scared, and I don't blame him. It sounds as if Cy's about to tell him something terrifying. I kind of wish now that I'd told Gary myself, so he was prepared, and so he wouldn't say anything awful to Cyrus. Because if he does, I won't be able to like him anymore either.

"What?" Gary says. "Just tell me."

I hold my breath as Cyrus stands up and paces from one side of the room to the other. Finally he stops and stares right at Gary. "I'm pretty sure . . . I'm gay," he says.

Gary doesn't say anything for a few seconds, and then he shrugs. "Okay. I didn't know. Thanks for telling me."

I breathe again. Pretty good so far.

"You're only the second person I've told," Cy says.

Gary nods. "You told Maisie."

"Yeah," Cy says. "I mean, I just figured it out myself."

"Right," Gary says. "I won't say anything if you don't want me to. I know people can be mean sometimes. I told you about my cousin Max, right? Some kids at his school were pretty awful to him when Max first came out, but his real friends were okay with it—most of them, anyway."

Cy seems to be breathing again too. "Yeah? I'm glad to hear that. And you still like him? Your cousin?"

Gary gives a sharp laugh. "Of course I still like him."

"Cool. That's really cool."

"It would be pretty crappy to stop liking somebody just because he was gay," Gary says. "Did you think I wouldn't want to be your friend anymore, Cy?"

Cyrus doesn't look at Gary. "I . . . I wasn't sure."

"Well, you can be sure. It doesn't matter to me. Okay?"

"Okay," Cy says, sneaking a quick peek at Gary's face.

I'm so happy about Gary's response, I can't stop smiling. He's as nice a person as I thought he was. (Now if I could just ignore the part of my brain that's screaming, *And he wants me to be his girlfriend!*)

"Great," I say, hoping Cy has revealed all he's going to. "Now that the big secret's out and we're all cool with it, let's get back to working on the script."

"Um, one more thing," Cy says.

He looks at me for encouragement, but after what happened this afternoon, I'm pretty sure the whole truth will only make all three of us feel terrible. I stare at Cy and hope he can read my face. *Don't do it.* An hour and a half ago, I kissed Gary. I don't think he's going to fulfill Cy's dreams *and* mine.

But Gary's looking at him, waiting for the one more thing.

Cyrus turns from me to Gary, and for a minute I'm afraid he's falling into those dark eyes just like I did. But finally Cy pulls his gaze away and flops into a chair as if he's a stuffed toy, as if his muscles have turned to oatmeal and he can't hold himself up anymore. Did he get my message? Or did he just get scared?

"Um, maybe if your cousin comes to visit some-time, I could meet him," Cy says quietly. "I don't really know any other gay people. Kids, I mean."

"Good idea," Gary says. "Max and his family usually come for a weekend during the summer. I'll make sure you meet him."

Cy looks so small in that big chair, I want to go over and squash in beside him like we did when we were little kids. I want to tell him *I* love him, no matter what, but I know it's not the same, and it won't take away the ache he's feeling.

Cyrus forces the corners of his mouth to curl up slightly. "Is there any more of that iced tea in the fridge?" he asks.

"Oh, sure," Gary says. "I'll get you some."

But Cy jumps up first and gallops out of the room. "Never mind. I can get it," he calls back over his shoulder. I'm guessing there's a tear he wants to let slide down his cheek unnoticed.

After a few seconds Gary turns and looks down the couch to where I'm huddled in the opposite corner. He gives me a minuscule smile and says softly, "It's me, isn't it? That's the other thing Cy was going to say."

I can't tell him, of course, but I return his smile, and he nods.

"Okay," he says. "I get it now. Why you can't be my girlfriend."

I clear my throat. "You know what? Sometime we should watch *Blade Runner*. I'd probably like it more the second time."

★34★

"Have you got the bone ready?" I yell.

Cy is standing on the far side of my backyard. "Got it!" He waves the marrow-stuffed dog treat in the air.

"Remember," Gary says, "as soon as she gets to you, snap the leash back on her."

"I will," Cy says.

I get the camera positioned correctly on the tripod so it will catch Gary and me and Buffy (called Hildegarde in the movie) as we streak across the yard toward Cyrus. Later, I can edit out the part where Buffy gets her treat, so it looks like she's just running loose. The late afternoon light is just as I imagined it—our shadows will race ahead of us like they're ghosts too. I turn the camera on and run back to stand beside Gary, who's holding on to Buffy/Hildegarde by the ruff of her neck.

Cy and Gary and I have pretty much figured out how to be friends without feeling too weird about who likes who. After Cy told Gary he's gay, Cy got me alone and thanked me for not becoming Gary's girlfriend.

"I know you like him a lot," he said, "and I feel bad about that. But really, Maze, I don't think I could be around the two of you if . . ."

"If he was my boyfriend?"

He nodded. "It would hurt too much."

"I know," I said. "It's okay. I don't need a boyfriend. I'm *twelve*."

"I keep thinking maybe someday . . . I mean, you never know what might happen in the future, do you?" Cyrus looked hopeful.

"That's for sure," I agreed. I guess Cy meant that maybe someday Gary would like him as more than a friend, but I was thinking that when we get older, Cyrus might find a different boy who'd love him back.

Once in a while when the three of us are hanging out together, Cy gets a sorrowful look on his face, especially if Gary smiles at me. And sometimes when Gary and I look at each other, I wish I could have a second kiss, but then I remember that Mr. Schmitz eventually got his second dance with Grandma. I can wait. I just hope I don't have to wait fifty years.

"Action!" I yell.

Cyrus waves Buffy's bone in the air, and Gary lets her go. She takes off loping across the yard as planned, and Gary and I run after her, laughing madly because we've just scared the daylights out of someone (in a scene we haven't shot yet, with an actor we still need to cast).

"Who knew being a ghost would be so much fun!" I yell to Gary/Vincent.

"Aren't you glad Hildegarde was in the car when we died, Adeline?" Gary/Vincent says. "She's the scariest one of us all!"

I give my most evil laugh, and we run out of the frame. "Cut! We got it!" I yell, then turn to see Buffy leap for the bone in Cyrus's hand and knock him over in her reckless rush to get it in her mouth.

"Hey!" Cy yells. He grabs the white buffalo around the neck, but I can tell he's having trouble getting the leash hooked on.

"I can't—" he says, and then Hildegarde is suddenly free. She dances around for a minute with the bone in her mouth and takes off running.

"Get her before she knocks over the camera!" Cy shouts.

She's headed right for the tripod, but Gary and I are ready. Gary lunges for his misbehaving pooch just as she runs right under the mounted camera.

The entire thing, tripod and all, flies up in the air, and in the most athletic move of my entire life, I fall underneath them and catch the camera in my hands. Okay, it actually hits me in the shoulder, but then I get hold of it with my hands and it's not broken into a million pieces. I also take a tripod pole to the stomach, but it's a small price to pay. Gary lands on Buffy, and Cyrus runs over with the leash. Of course, by then Buffy's lying down in the grass, munching on her bone, her brown spots no longer covered up, baby powder sprinkling the grass behind her.

I look over the camera. "It seems fine," I say. "That was close, though."

"Sorry, guys," Cy says. "She's hard to pin down when she wants to run."

"I think we're going to have to limit Hildegarde's scenes," I say. "She's funny, but she's dangerous."

Gary nods and points to my white jeans. "Also, our clothes are grass-stained and we've sweated off most of our makeup."

"We'll have to bleach our costumes before we can shoot another scene," I say.

Cy folds up the tripod. "Can we make this movie, or not? Maybe it's too complicated."

"It's definitely harder than I thought it would be," Gary says. "Buffy's not much of an actor."

I stare at them as they brush off their clothes. "Are you kidding me? Do you know how hard it was to make *The African Queen?*" We're seeing it tomorrow at the Lincoln, and I've been reading up on it. "It rained so much that they couldn't shoot for days, and there were wild animals and poisonous snakes and scorpions, and the water was so bad that Katharine Hepburn got dysentery, and—"

Gary laughs. "Okay, okay. When you put it that way—"

Cy looks horrified. "I'm never making a movie with you in the jungle, so don't even ask me," he says. "It's one thing to wrestle Buffy, but no movie is worth dealing with snakes and scorpions."

Gary is tying Buffy's leash to the leg of the picnic table when we hear Mom's car pull into the driveway.

"They're home!" Cy yells, and we take off for the back door. Cyrus and Gary are as excited as I am about Grandma and Mr. Schmitz taking a trip to the county courthouse this afternoon. How often does one of your grandparents get married?

Inside, Mom is already kicking off her heels, while Dad pulls off his tie. Neither of them likes dressing up much. Grandma, who's keeping all her clothes on, looks really pretty in a flowered pink dress.

"Where's your new husband?" I ask her.

She doesn't look the least bit confused by my question. "Hank stopped at the bakery to pick up our cake," she says. "Wait till you see what we got. Chocolate cake with strawberry icing!" She looks as happy as a little kid at a birthday party.

"I have to change out of these duds," Mom says. "It's too hot for anything but shorts."

I follow her into her bedroom, hoping to talk to her alone for a minute. "Is it okay if Cyrus and Gary stay for dinner?" I ask.

"Sure," Mom says. "Cy's parents are coming over too. Dad is grilling chicken, and I made potato salad and deviled eggs this morning. There should be plenty."

I figured Mom would be okay with adding a few people to the celebration, since she started working again last week. She doesn't like the job that much, but the hours are flexible and she works from home, which is good if she needs to be with Grandma when Mr. Schmitz is busy. She makes calls for a big roofing company in St. Louis, trying to talk people into getting an estimate on a new roof. Half the time they hang up on her, but she gets paid whether they buy a roof or not.

Mom steps into her closet to take off her dress and pull on shorts. "Did your uncle call while we were gone?" she asks.

"I don't think so," I say. "Is he supposed to?"

"We haven't heard from him in weeks. I emailed him that his mother was getting married today. I assumed he'd call." I hate that she always sounds so aggravated when she talks about Uncle Walt. Sometimes it seems like she knows a different person than I do.

"He'll probably call. You just got back," I say.

Mom laughs as she comes out of the closet. "I should know better than to complain about him to you."

I sit on her bed and watch her brush her hair. "Did you like Uncle Walt more when you were kids?"

She stops brushing and looks at me. "It was always a complicated thing, Maisie, because of the way Grandma worshipped him. I knew she loved me too, but not in the same way, and I couldn't help feeling jealous. I did like Walt, though, more than I wanted to. And probably for the same reasons you do. He was smart and funny, and he made me laugh. But, Maisie, adults have to be responsible for more than just having a good time."

"He's trying to be more responsible, Mom," I say quietly.

"I know you think so," she says. "I hope you're right."

She gets down on her knees to look for her flip-flops under the bed.

"Mom? Will you be mad at me if I leave New Aztec when I grow up? If I move to Los Angeles to try to be a filmmaker?"

She leans back on her heels and looks at me. "You know you have to go to college first, right?"

"I know. I want to go to college."

"You'd better. I put money aside for it every month."

"You do?"

She nods. "Of course. I want you to have your chance, Maisie. Dad wants that too. Once you finish college, you can decide what you want to do with your life."

"I think I'll still want to go to Los Angeles, but I feel like I'll be a bad person if I leave New Aztec. If I leave you and Dad." Just saying it makes me tear up a little.

Mom sits next to me on the bed and puts her arm around me. "Leaving New Aztec doesn't make you good or bad. Neither does staying here. Life is full of choices, Maisie, and all of them have a plus side and a minus side. You have to weigh it all out and then decide. And just because you make a decision doesn't mean you can't change your mind later."

I lean into her side. "Okay."

She gives me a squeeze. "You don't have to decide today. You've got time."

"Thanks, Mom."

"Now hand me my flip-flops and let's start celebrating," she says. "And maybe you should film a little bit tonight. So we'll have it . . . later."

"Really? You want me to?"

She smiles. "Yes, Hitchcock, I really do."

In the dining room Mr. Schmitz pours champagne
for the grown-ups and sparkling cider for us kids.
I get some footage of everybody toasting Grandma
and Mr. Schmitz. Dad gets a little weepy and says,
"May it last forever!" and then Mom kisses him,
which I also get on film, more or less accidentally.
I pan over to the table with the cake box.

"Can I see the cake, Mr. Schmitz?" I ask. "I
want to get a shot of it before it gets cut."

He gives me a long look. "Yes, you can, but I
think you should stop calling me Mr. Schmitz."

Does he want me to call him Grandpa now? I'm
not sure I can do that.

"Call me Hank. That's what my friends call
me," he says.

"Am I your friend now?" I've never had a friend
as old as Mr. . . . . Hank.

"I'm afraid you are, Maisie. Whether you like it or not."

I decide I like it. I put down the camera in order to sneak a fingerful of pink icing from the side of the cake, even though we haven't had dinner yet. Hank doesn't say a word.

Dad is getting out the chicken to put on the grill when the phone rings. I run to get it.

"Hey, Hitchcock!" Uncle Walt sings out my name.

"It's Uncle Walt!" I yell, and the people who've wandered out to the kitchen come back into the dining room.

"Is everybody there?" he asks. "Your parents and Grandma and all?"

"Yeah, we're all here. Hank too. And Cyrus and Gary."

"Put me on speakerphone. I've got news!"

I hit the button and put the phone on the table. "Okay, we're all listening," I say.

"Hey, everybody!" The phone vibrates a little on the table, as if it's excited too.

Most of us say hi back, but Grandma looks around, confused. "Walter? Where are you?"

"He's on the phone, Ma," Mom tells her. "There, on the table."

"Ma!" Uncle Walt yells. "Did you take the plunge? Are you married?"

Grandma's face turns as pink as her dress. "I'm a bride for the second time!" she says. Hank moves in next to her, and she loops her arm around his waist.

"Congratulations to you both," Uncle Walt says. "Hank, you finally landed her."

"It was worth the wait," Hank says.

Is there a word that means glad and sad at the same time? That's the way I feel when I see how Hank looks at Grandma. I loved my grandpa, but I almost wish Grandma had married Hank fifty years ago, so he didn't have to spend most of his life being such an unhappy grouch.

"You said you had news," I remind Uncle Walt.

"Yes, I do. It's not exactly the news I was hoping to be able to tell you, but it's not bad. I didn't get the part I wanted in that TV pilot, but—"

I cut him off. "What? How come? That's not fair! You would have been perfect!"

He laughs. "I wish everybody had as much confidence in me as you do, Hitch. But listen, I got a different part. It's not as big, but it's okay. At this point it's more of a recurring role, but if I do a good job, I could become a regular. And if the show is a hit—"

"The pilot has to get picked up first, doesn't it?" Mom asks.

"Of course. And that's not a done deal, but it's

looking good. We started filming the pilot this week, and there's been a lot of interest in it. I wish I could tell you I had the lead, but hey, it's a job, and I'm glad to have it."

I know he wanted this show to be his big break. So did I. Even though he's saying this is good news, I can hear the disappointment underneath the cheerfulness.

"I know they'll make you a regular cast member, Uncle Walt," I say, "once they see how great you are."

"We'll see, kiddo. Keep your fingers crossed."

Grandma puts her face down near the phone. "What does it mean, honey?" she asks. "Are you coming home soon?"

"Well, no, Ma, I won't be home for a while. I'm not sure when the next time will be."

"I'm happy for you, sweetheart," Grandma says. "I miss you, but I'm happy for you."

"Me too," Mom says finally. "I'm sorry it wasn't the part you wanted, but we'll hope for the best."

"Thanks, Cindy," Uncle Walt says. "You know, I wanted to be able to tell you I was finally getting a big paycheck. I was hoping I could send money so you could go back to school, to finish your music degree. I still want to do that. I hope someday I'll be able to."

Mom opens her mouth, but no words come out.

"Cin? Are you there?"

"She's here," Dad says, putting an arm around Mom's shoulders. "She just can't talk."

Finally Mom sputters to life. "Walter, that's very nice of you, but you don't need to—"

"I do need to. I want to. And I promise you I'm not going to forget about it. I want you to have your big break too."

Mom's chin starts to quiver and a tear runs down her cheek, but I'm pretty sure that this time it's happy crying.

"And the other thing I've been thinking is I want to get Maisie out here, to show her around LA. I should be able to come up with the plane fare by next summer. What do you think, Hitch? A week or two in LA, just you and me, taking in the sights."

"Really? Yes, yes!" I can't believe it. Me, in LA!

"We'll go to some studios. I'll get us onto a set. My apartment is small, but you wouldn't mind a sleeping bag on the floor, would you?"

"Are you kidding? I'll sleep outside in a tent if I have to!"

I'm jumping up and down and high-fiving Cyrus and Gary, but Mom manages to stop crying long enough to put a damper on my excitement. "Let's not make too many plans too far ahead. We'll see what next summer brings."

The phone gets quiet for a minute, and then Uncle Walt says, "Cindy, let Maisie come. I want to show her it's worth it to follow her dreams."

"Is it, Walter?" Mom says, but she says it quietly, as if she's really asking.

"I think it is, Cin."

Mom doesn't say anything else, but she nods.

Grandma bends near the phone again. "Walter, have you met Hank? You'd really like him."

"I did meet Hank, Ma. Remember? When I was in New Aztec."

"Now when was that, sweetheart?"

Hank interrupts her. "Walt, we sure wish you were here to eat some of this pink cake with us!"

"And drink the champagne too," Grandma says.

"I'll drink champagne here and raise a glass to the two of you," Uncle Walt says.

"We'll drink a toast to you too, Walter," Mom says quietly. "A toast to following your dreams."

Dinner is exceptionally tasty, although we're all in such a good mood that we probably wouldn't care if the chicken was burned to cinders and the potato salad was moldy. Cy and Gary stay late, and we talk about how much fun I'm going to have in Los Angeles with Uncle Walt next summer. I wish they could come too, but they're being good sports about it, which doesn't surprise me. They're the two best friends a girl could have.

So, I guess this is the end for now, or at least it's a good stopping point. It might not be a perfect ending, but it's a pretty happy one. Anyway, it's as good as in *Pretty in Pink,* when Duckie doesn't end up with Andie but you just know he's not giving up on her *that* easily. Everybody deserves at least one happy ending. Grandma and Hank got one. And I think there are a few more out there for the rest of us.

THE END (FOR NOW)

★ Movies Referenced ★

(in the order they appear in the text)

The Martian (2015)
Inside Out (2015)
Casablanca (1942)
Frozen (2013)
Raiders of the Lost Ark (1981)
Butch Cassidy and the Sundance Kid (1969)
Monty Python and the Holy Grail (1975)
Pirates of the Caribbean (2006)
Blade Runner (1982)
The Perks of Being a Wallflower (2012)
The NeverEnding Story (1984)
The Matrix (1999)
Star Wars: The Force Awakens (2015)
The Princess Bride (1987)
The King and I (1956)
South Pacific (1958)
Roman Holiday (1953)
Cat on a Hot Tin Roof (1958)
2001: A Space Odyssey (1968)
The Godfather (1972)
Back to the Future (1985)
The Breakfast Club (1985)
Adam's Rib (1949)
His Girl Friday (1940)
The Jerk (1979)
Edward Scissorhands (1990)
Psycho (1960)
The Birds (1963)

Vertigo (1958)
Napoleon Dynamite (2004)
Harold and Maude (1971)
Ferris Bueller's Day Off (1986)
Harvey (1950)
The Sound of Music (1965)
Groundhog Day (1993)
To Kill a Mockingbird (1962)
Dirty Dancing (1987)
Dracula (1931)
Moonstruck (1987)
Doctor Zhivago (1965)
Lady and the Tramp (1955)
Mrs. Doubtfire (1993)
Dead Poets Society (1989)
The Grand Budapest Hotel (2014)
East of Eden (1955)
E.T. (1982)
The Birdcage (1996)
The Adventures of Priscilla, Queen of the Desert
    (1994)
Philadelphia (1993)
Brokeback Mountain (2005)
Toy Story 3 (2010)
Rebel Without a Cause (1955)
Bringing Up Baby (1938)
Sixteen Candles (1984)
Tootsie (1982)
A League of Their Own (1992)
Frankenstein (1931)
Big (1988)
Rear Window (1954)
The African Queen (1951)
Pretty in Pink (1986)

★ Acknowledgments ★

When I was a kid, my uncle Walt was always on the road, playing his trombone with big bands in Chicago, New York, and Los Angeles, where he finally settled. Once or twice a year, he'd fly home to small-town Illinois—the only person we knew who'd actually been on an airplane—and my grandmother and I would rejoice. For my mother, her brother's arrival was less of a celebration. She was the one who shouldered the responsibility of their increasingly needy parents while Walt was off following his dreams.

I see now that Walt wasn't perfect, but at the time I idolized and adored him. His life was so large and so exciting, and when he was around, that excitement infected me. He was the only person I knew who had chosen a life in the arts, and I believe, without a doubt, that he is the reason I had the audacity to think I could do the same. This book is for him. Every kid needs an Uncle Walt to inspire them; for those who don't have one, please feel free to borrow Maisie's.

My writer-friends in two critique groups have been with me through success and struggle. Thank you always: Pat Lowery Collins, Liza Ketchum, Nancy Werlin, Lisa Papademetriou, Jane Yolen, Patricia MacLachlan, Lesléa Newman, Ann Turner, Barbara Diamond Goldin, and Corinne Demas. I also depend on the advice and support of Elise Broach, Chris Tebbetts, Heather Knight Richard, Jeannine Atkins, Jo Knowles, and Cindy Faughnan.

Two very different organizations have supported me over the years, one financially, both emotionally. The Fine Arts Work Center in Provincetown, Massachusetts, has been home and family to me for more than forty years. I may well have given up on my dreams had I not washed up on their shore so long ago. And Kindling Words, the writing retreat for children's book authors and illustrators, has been a lifeline for me for thirty years. The Fine Arts Work Center and Kindling Words laid the foundation on which I built a writing career.

Thanks, of course, to Yolanda Scott and Karen Boss, who've been champions for this book, and to everyone at Charlesbridge Publishing, in particular the amazing copy-editor, Josette Haddad. And to Ginger Knowlton, agent and cheerleader, whose encouragement keeps me afloat.